A Dilli-Mumbai  Story

... When Love Won Over Terror

A Dilli-Mumbai

Story

... When Love Won Over Terror

Abhimanyu Jha

Srishti
PUBLISHERS & DISTRIBUTORS

Srishti Publishers & Distributors
N-16, C. R. Park
New Delhi 110 019
editorial@srishtipublishers.com

First published by
Srishti Publishers & Distributors in 2011
Sixth impression 2015

All characters in this book are fictitious, and any resemblance to real persons, living or dead, is coincidental.

Printed and bound in India

Dedicated,

To Mummy and Papa who developed in me the love of reading.

To Didi and Sekhar whose love, support and guidance helped me write.

To all the people who continue to live their wonderful lives despite the horrors of terrorism.

To sweet romance that often makes the world go round.

Acknowledgements

I would like to thank my friend Mona for her invaluable feedback and suggestions without which this book would not have become what it is.

I would like to thank Richa for being the first person to read the manuscript in entirety and giving a response that prevented a premature heart attack in the author.

I would like to thank Karthik, Indu, Bhargavi, Harvinder, Sumon, Kisalaya, Prof. M S Sriram and my other friends from IIT Madras and IIM Ahmedabad who first recognized and told me that I could write stuff that others may want to read (and definitely read if I promised them a million bucks).

I would like to thank Carina, Abraham, Ruth, Heena, Sushmita, Deepa, Pammi Di, Sanjib Jijaji and many others who waddled bravely through the numerous samples of the written word that I thrust below their noses now and then.

I would like to thank my friends and colleagues from my company TalentBridge, especially Gaurav, Sandip, Yayati, Rahul and Prem for their encouragement and support while writing this book.

I would like to thank my friend and author Sidin for the first expert review and Tanushree for designing the cover of this book.

I would like to thank my family and numerous friends who faithfully responded to my questions on the best title, design, ending etc and helped me spread the word about this book.

I would like to thank the survivors of the 2008 Mumbai attacks especially Bruce Hanna and Bhisham Mansukhani whose stories posted on internet sites gave me the idea and the background material for this book.

I would like to thank my publisher Srishti for bringing this book to the world and making me knowledgeable about the niceties of publishing.

Grateful acknowledgment is also made for reprinting a teeny weeny bit of material previously published: Harper Collins Publishers Inc: Excerpt from *Slowness* by Milan Kundera. Copyright © 1995 by Milan Kundra. Translation © 1996 by Linda Asher.

And finally, immense thanks to late genius Erich Segal - who sent me into a lovelorn, and-the-sun-will-never-shine kind of depression when I was fifteen - for giving me inspiration for this *love story.*

Because, in some other universe, you are me, I am you,
And we are perfectly happy together; or perhaps not, and
Just like this…

Mumbai, Nov 27, 2008

Let Apu live.

Who knows where is she now? Meters or centimeters away from the terrorists? And I can do nothing. *Nothing.*

Please god. You gave us so little time. We have so much to do, live for. She was the prettiest girl I had met, soon after we met. You know that. *My saanwli memsaab…*

Don't let her....

But why would god listen? It's not he who's let her down. If I weren't such a bastard, would she be here today? Who pushed her at death's door?

Acting as if I was the one to save the world, when I can't even save her.

Delhi, 2003

The year St. Stephen's accepted me as a student of economics, Aarushi turned fifteen, developed hideous taste in music, and became unbearable. She had been on my neck the whole day, and day before, and day before… to go with her to a music show in IIT. I had done my best to avoid her - first I hid from her, and then ignored her plaintive calls of 'Bhaiya'. Then I remembered her sixteenth birthday was coming in two weeks and a sense of brotherly duty washed over me.

So about seven in the evening, I stopped teasing her by pretending I wasn't going anywhere from my blissful recliner/flatscreen combo where I was enjoying Andre Agassi cream some unknown dude in a French Open match. We decided I would run ahead and buy tickets for the show while she followed with a couple of her giggly and irritating friends (my private opinion; one of them Ira had even declared love for me on a *violet* letterhead!).

My Ducati 996 waited for me in the driveway, newly washed by its proud owner. Sexy black babe. I patted her butt, flicked a speck of dust off her muscular haunches (how dare the speck!), then revved her up. She purred, roared, and in the sinful lap of the V-twin, I was off in a flash.

I arrived at IIT main gate in eleven minutes, twenty-nine seconds. For our biking fraternity that would be an unspeakable crime - I plead in my defense I could have made it in less than five if it was not for the bloody blooming buzzing traffic.

Anyway, as I was picking up speed after rounding the circle near the girl's hostel, a puppy suddenly ran in front of my bike from the right.

There was no time to remember and apply the four stage braking drill; I forgot the nuances I had so attentively learnt in a workshop not months ago and filled in a notebook 64 pages thick. I swerved and gave all that I had got to the front brake – together.

Another, bigger crime. Expectedly, my baby gave me the middle finger, the front wheel locked up, tucked under, and we both went skidding up the road. Meanwhile, I had the good sense to ball myself and roll off her before she dragged me along and her weight made keema of my left leg.

Event Horizon!

When I lifted my chin off the ground, I found myself staring at the toes of a pair of pretty feet clad in Kolhapuri chappals. Wow! The privilege of examining a feminine feet up, close and personal! Meaning it was impossible not to minutely notice the beige nail polish and the yellow toe-ring with silver beads on the third toe. Further inspection was interrupted by the owner who bent down to help me stand up and asked me: "Are you ok?"

It was a charming voice. As I stood up and my eyes moved up her body, I noticed other attributes in this order: white salwar, white kameez streaked with red, hennaed hand with yellow bangles and the same beige nail polish I had noticed on the toes, long hair, svelte figure, red dupatta, nice… Politely, I removed my eyes from the round, tantalizing pair upwards… silvery necklace, full lips, nose a little flared, brown eyes with large lashes, and eyebrows like mine – slightly curving out, then smoothing down. My assister was definitely pretty, and had a liking for super large ear rings.

The scoundrel who had caused all this, the cute puppy, was squealing in excitement a few feet away. "Thanks. I am fine," I told her. "Your puppy?"

She didn't answer the puppy question, and instead, concentrated on demolishing my confidence about my fineness. The next second she let out a cry, jerking her pretty head to the right. "Shit!"

What! *What*?

"Look at that! Looks bad!" Kolhapuri chappals said pointing at my left arm.

Usually, I wear my protective gear; and a leather jacket is compulsory among them. You aren't a biker if you go out without one. But today wasn't a normal day. Aarushi had bugged me for so long that to escape the torture, I had pulled on whatever I could reach from my recliner (in this case a bottle green Polo neck) and run for the bike.

Meaning my arms were left naked, so when I followed the direction of the pretty stranger's fingers, I found myself staring at a gash on my left arm, brimming with bright, red blood.

Crap! I was not feeling the wound, not even a little. Must be due to a sharp pebble or nail that I had dragged my arm over while rolling. Singularly unlucky because apart from that one gash, I had not split a single hair. Duniya bananewale, kahe ko Murphy's Law banayi!

"No, the puppy's not mine." Kolhapuri chappals looked into my eyes with concern. "But I do have antiseptic and bandages in my room. Is it hurting bad?"

For a second, I was tempted to take her up on her offer. I had never seen an IIT room before, much less a feminine one (what did they look like? Mini – spaceships, with computers and kaleidoscopic screens blinking all over?) But this girl looked like any other regular, pretty girl with a good heart. Nothing Dexterish about her – I couldn't for my life imagine her sweating over double or triple integrals.

And then, before Kolhapuri chappals and the IIT tag could snare me in their temptation, thankfully I remembered my black baby. She was lying wounded on the road, god knows in what state.

Shucks! I had to attend to her first.

"No, I am fine," I said declining the generous offer with a smile. "Thanks a lot. I will manage."

"Are you sure?"

I nodded, said thanks to Kolhapuri chappals once more, and walked over quickly to my Ducati. A couple of guys had crowded around the bike, admiring her. I proudly pulled my girl up, assisted by the guys who I bet were dying to get their hands on her. I let them; one should be generous sometimes.

My girl was ok. A little road-rashed, but nothing that couldn't be fixed. I heaved a sigh of relief, patted a little to comfort her, and mounted her.

Then on an instinct, I looked back. Kolhapuri chappals stood at the same place, gazing at me. The puppy was now by her side, still squealing. She shouted when our eyes met. "Everything's ok?"

I nodded vigorously at her. "Yup, all is well." And took off.

Mumbai, Nov 27, 2008, 12:38 AM

As we were on our way back to Rohan's house, my phone rang. Apu! My eyes burned. "Apu… apu… sweety. Can you hear me… APU?"

"Yes, I can hear you," she whispered.

"How are you?"

"How else? Crouching with everyone on the floor of the best hotel of India." Even now, I could hear a tinge of mirth in her voice. "Wow! Am I in a real thriller! We dodged bullets and grenades and all."

"Are you ok?"

"Yes. Never felt better."

I almost snapped at her for misplaced humor before remembering where and how she was. I controlled myself with effort. "Apu, don't joke now. Please baby. Are you completely fine? No wounds… nothing?"

There was a second's hesitation. Then a "yes". It was a feeble yes. She was lying.

"Don't lie! What happened? Tell the truth. *Please.*"

Rohan, driving beside me, gestured me to calm down.

"It's not going to help Ani!" she insisted. "You will worry needlessly. I am pretty close to being fine."

"I want to know! What happened?"

There was a little pause. Then Apu started in a measured voice. "It's a slight gash on the shoulder. Even smaller than the one you got when you fell of your bike at my feet, so don't worry. Don't know how I got it. Shrapnel probably. We have tied it up for now with whatever we could get."

"Is it bleeding?"

"Stupid," Apu said laughing. "Don't worry. I am fine. People around me and the hotel staff… everyone is very helpful. Zero worries. All I need to do is practice crouching well, and I will be home safe and sound."

Suddenly there was a loud noise in the background. My heart jumped! "APU!"

Her voice became very soft and urgent. "Baby I have to go now. Something's big exploded… and we can hear voices outside. I promise I will be safe. Don't worry. Bye baby, love you…"

"Apu… APU!" But the phone was cut.

Delhi, 2003

About half an hour after I fell of my bike and came face to feet with Kolhapuri chappals, I got the gash on my arm stitched and bandaged. Dr. Awasthi, a family friend who lived in Hauz Khas close by, helped me out in exchange for ten minutes of passionate gyan over safe riding. "Get a bike suitable for Delhi roads, not Monte Carlo!" he scolded me.

I nodded meekly. It's prudent not to argue with doctors who are stitching you up.

But the medical attention had made me late. By the time I returned to IIT campus, Aarushi's gumbal had already arrived and was waiting for the tickets. I parked my bike and made a dash for the ticketing line.

When I reached the ticket counter, I got a pleasant surprise. Kolhapuri chappals was the ticket seller!

"Hi!" I beamed, glad to see her again.

"Hi," she beamed back. She looked down at my stitches. "You fine now?"

I said I was. And I was sorry for refusing her hospitality, but I thought I needed a grumpy doctor than a kind engineer.

"That's ok," she said. "I wouldn't get stitched by me either." Then she returned to the matter at hand. "Tickets?"

"Yep, five. Give me whichever are priced highest."

Her eyebrows knit. "Priced highest?" She smiled thinly. "Why? To go along with your highest priced bike?"

Then it dawned on me that the blunt way in which I had asked for highest priced tickets, along with my flashy bike, may look to her as if I was flaunting my wealth! Crud!

"No, it's for my younger sister," I replied hastily. "Her birthday is in two weeks and she is crazy about the band."

"Oh! Where is she?"

"There," I said pointing in the general direction where Aarushi was. "In the highest priced car," I said grinning.

Kolhapuri chappals grinned back. "Is that so? Cool. Five tickets right? One for you, one for your sister, and three for the bike?"

I didn't take the bait. "Yep," I said with lips pursed.

"Then give me three thousand seven hundred and fifty for five *highest priced tickets*," she said emphasizing the last three words.

Wicked girl! I glanced at the price list. It showed something else. "I thought the highest priced tickets were a thousand each. Shouldn't it be five thousand then?"

"The thousand tickets are not for everyone. Only for special guests."

"Ain't I special?" I ribbed her. "Got highest priced bike, car, everything..."

I could sense that Kolhapuri chappals was searching for a biting retort, but she didn't have time - the people behind me were getting impatient as the show had started. "Enjoy the show," she simply said and thrust the tickets in my hand. I guess the mild violence of the move was an indication of her dissatisfaction with the current state of affairs. I turned away elated at having won the verbal duel.

The show was bad. For me.

Aarushi and gang, on the other hand, were having the time of their lives – screaming, dancing and cheering. Kids!

Bored, I came out of the open air theatre in the middle to have a cigarette. That's when I saw Kolhapuri chappals again. She was still sitting at the ticket counter. But she was jobless now. Good.

Not long after, she turned her head in my direction and saw me. I was kind of hoping for that. She smiled. I waved. She waved back. I strolled towards her after putting off the cigarette and launching it into a nearby wastebasket.

"Done for the day?"

"Guess so," she replied. "Haven't sold a ticket in the last twenty minutes." A teasing grin appeared on her face. "How was the show from the highest priced seats?"

I grinned back. "Highest priced disappointment! By the way," I added, "you *didn't* give me the highest priced seats."

"Yep... because you aren't *special*," pat came the reply.

I wasn't about to let Kolhapuri chappals have the upper hand in the duel. Told her I *was* special. "Explained to you why," I reminded her, "and you couldn't say anything back."

She protested. "I knew what to say. I just didn't."

"Why?"

"Thought it would sound rude."

I told her I didn't believe her. She shrugged her shoulders.

"Ok, I will get you coffee if you can tell it to me right now."

"We don't get good coffee here. The incentive is weak."

I was stumped. "That's not..."

"But a coke will do. We do get good coke in our canteen. They can't mess *that* up."

"Ok, I'll get you a whole crate of coke! But what is it?"

"You really want to know?"

"*Yes!*"

"Well... I wanted to say you aren't special here," she said, "because here... we measure worth by the size of your brains, not by the size of your pockets."

In the Canteen

When Kolhapuri chappals told me I wasn't special because of the size of my brains, displaying a pride that was perhaps typical of her collegemates, I was tempted to tell her a fact very few people knew about me. That even if we went by the size of brains, or to be precise the intelligence contained in it, I would be considered special anywhere. Even here in IIT. I would outrace most or all IITians where IQ was concerned. Because I had an IQ of 153. They say Einstein's was about 160. That would be just seven more than me.

But I kept my mouth shut. My Ducati and my 6' 1" height was enough to impress or intimidate most people. I didn't want to bring my IQ in on top of that.

While we were having coke in the IIT canteen, the first thing Kolhapuri chappals said that she was sorry.

"Huh?"

"I shouldn't have said what I said," she said, her face troubled. "It must have sounded extremely rude. I didn't really mean it."

I told her it was ok. I knew she was joking, or rather trying to one up me in a war of words. And anyway, it wouldn't affect me because I myself wasn't too bad in the brains department.

"Aha?" She was interested.

I shrugged. "Topper of my school. Studying Economics at St. Stephens. That's not IIT, but that's… something."

"It is," she agreed. "And I don't know your name yet."

"Aniruddha Hirani. You?"

She said before she revealed her name, I had to promise I wouldn't laugh. I replied I *would* laugh. She was astonished at my reply, so I explained that would get us even – insult for insult. She smiled and said fine, I could laugh.

"So what's it?" I asked.

She swallowed once, then said: "Aparajita Pinto."

"What?"

"You *heard* me. I am a Goan Catholic whose mom loved her Bengali neighbors, *and* their Satyajit Ray movie collection. I am named after the second movie of the Apu trilogy."

"Ok, I won't laugh. But I actually like your name."

"Like it? At least it is Aparajita Pinto now. In school, I was called *Aparajito* Pinto! Which led to some creative interpretations like Jinto Pinto. I had a great time!"

I grinned. "Aparajita. Doesn't it mean 'the unbeatable'?"

"Yep."

"Are you?"

"I thought you experienced that just now, no?" She raised her eyebrows in an impish smile. "Anyway, I am Apu to my friends. It's much easier to pronounce."

Delhi,

On 21st Nov evening, ten of them left Karachi in a boat and traveled for thirty-eight hours. No one in the world except a few knew about them. They each had 6 to 7 magazines of 30 rounds plus 400 rounds not loaded in magazines, 8 hand grenades, one AK-47 assault rifle, an automatic loading revolver, credit cards and supply of dry fruits. On 23rd November, they hijacked an Indian trawler, killed four fishermen, and ordered the captain to sail to India. They reached within 4 nautical miles of Mumbai and killed the captain too. They then boarded three inflatable speedboats and sped towards Colaba, Mumbai.

They were coming for Apu.

Delhi, 2003

If there was a (and only) buddy my age I could trust my life with, it was Rohan. He had got two things better than me. Knowledge of bikes. And quality of heart. Not medically - he was slightly on the heavier side. Emotionally.

I told him about Apu when we were returning from our baski practice the next day.

"Umm… I met a girl yesterday," I informed him.

He jerked his head towards me, eye brows arched, and let out a low, drawn out whistle. "You…"

"Keep your eyes on the road dude!" I had to cut him off. We were in his car and were dangerously close to hitting a scooter. "I definitely don't want go to jail *today*."

"Sorry!" He turned his eyes back on the road. "But I thought you had stopped liking girls."

"What?" Then I got his drift and ribbed him back: "Dude, it's not me who drools after rugged old men!"

That was a standing joke between us. Rohan liked Harley Davidsons; I preferred my Ducati. I had told him Harleys were like rugged old men of the sea (figuratively), while Ducatis were like the long legged beauties of Baywatch. In short, he rode rugged old men, while I rode Pam Anderson kinda sexy babes. And that made him…

The joke never failed to get to him. He shook his head. "Dude, I have said a million times that's a horrible comparison. Anyway, ask Nisha if you aren't gay. She's dying for you and you don't –

"- Nisha is dying for half the North Campus… and *counting*!"

He chortled. "But you still are her first among equals. Anyway, what's her name – I mean the girl you met yesterday?"

"Aparajita."

"She does have a name! I thought you were bluffing about her. What's her number? I will totally believe you if you took her number."

"She doesn't have a number."

"So you're lying!"

I told him I was *not* lying, that the girl lived in IIT girl's hostel, that she didn't have her own number but the hostel had one, and that I had taken the hostel number. It was 01124746350. Was he satisfied now?

"011… She's given the STD code too. She isn't a Delhite?"

"No… she's from Goa."

"Goa! Aha! Beach girl. Are you going to call her?"

I replied I was still thinking.

"Still thinking? Why? Isn't she girlfriend material?"

I was surprised. He was seldom this aggressive. "She definitely is… Hey! Are you doubting she exists?"

Rohan turned his head slightly. "Dude, I am not doubting she exists… or that you met her. I am not even doubting that you want to call and meet her again. You mentioned her and are thinking of her… that's miracle enough! I am only doubting that you *will* call and meet her again. Some fifty girls in Delhi alone are pining for you, waiting for you to call. Now don't add Goa to the list of those states! Ok?"

Typical, senti Rohan. But he genuinely cared for me. I grinned at him. "Ok."

Though I wondered… would Apu be really pining for me? The thought made me strangely happy.

After reaching home, I scampered upstairs ignoring my mother's exhortations of coming down as soon as possible to have dinner, jumped on bed, punched 01124746350 in my cell phone, and asked for room 322. I sang a song for two minutes till Apu came on line and said "hi".

"Hi," I replied and stopped, testing if she would recognize my voice.

"Who's this?"

"Guess?"

There was a two seconds' pause. Then she said tonelessly: "What do you want Mr. Biker? I don't have any highest priced tickets anymore."

Happiness rushed through me. "But I have lots of coke. Want some?"

I thought I heard girls chanting in the background.

"When?"

Mumbai, Nov 27, 2008, 1:12 PM

Last SMS: Ani, my battry is gng 2 die anytme. Watever happns now, I luv u. A lot. Always. Apu.

Delhi, 2003

I stood outside Dilli Haat at 7:30 pm, drinking the most thanda coke in Delhi (according to my date) who beamed at me a *didn't I tell you so* smile. We were an illogically logical pair.

Wound back time to 6:30 pm. I arrived at IIT and managed to get to the Kailash girl's hostel without any mishap. I announced for Apu and sat in the lobby to wait for her. Twenty minutes later, she came down looking well… quite pretty in her pearl colored top and blue jeans with a pink tote hanging from her shoulder.

The one thing that hadn't changed since our first meeting, at least in size, were her earrings. They were still super large! But like a good date, I ignored her earrings, and politely asked her where she would like to go.

"Wherever we can get coke," she replied equally politely.

"Sure. Anything else besides that?"

"*Thanda* coke." She whispered loudly and huskily, making 'thanda' sound quite garam.

I swallowed. She seemed to be fixated on coke. I replied that while we would certainly have coke wherever we went, was there anything *else* she would like to have besides coke? Like pizza or kebab or sizzlers... those kind of things... if she got my drift.

"But you promised me coke!" she said.

I was confounded. Had I asked out a madwoman? Or more likely, she was taking my case by holding me to my words literally – hadn't I promised her coke? I decided to go along with her prank. I had no choice anyway - she was the lady in the pair!

So I asked her where would she like to have her coke.

Seemed she was waiting for this moment, ready with her answer. "Dilli Haat."

"Dilli Haat! Why only Dilli Haat?"

She answered with a non-sequitur. "Is this your first date?"

I was nonplussed. "Meaning?"

She replied that if I was asking *reasons* from a girl, it didn't look as if I had had much practice with them.

Even when I am down, I am not out. "But you are an IITian," I shot back. "You are supposed to be logical and all."

Did that sound lame? I hoped not.

It did I guess. "Tch... tch..," she clicked in reply. "I think you need lessons about girls. IITian or Italian, we are all the same. Illogically logical. *Nahin* samjhoge toh janoge."

Well... all I could say that for a Goan, her Hindi was quite good.

We came out of the hostel and walked towards my bike. Today I had brought my second bike, a British Racing Green Triumph Sprint ST. A 120 bhp, 75lb torque, 950 cc, 3 cylinder powerhouse. She was a tough babe with a twin spar aluminum chassis. And super sexy, though not as much as my Ducati. She came in Sapphire Blue and Tomato Red colors as well, but of the three sisters, I had liked the Green one best. The only catch was that at more than 200 kgs, she was no lightweight. Apu raised her eyebrows when she saw my green beauty.

"What's this?"

"My other bike. Triumph Sprint ST."

"So this is how you plan to triumph over me?"

Finally, my turn to give it back to her. "No, this is to take care of your butt."

Her eyes widened. "What?"

"The Ducati would have cramped your butt," I said with much amusement. "She is too uncomfy for the pillion rider. This girl is much easier on the butt."

Apu grinned. "Oh! Thanks for being so… so chivalrous about my butt! And… you call your bikes 'girl'?"

"Yup," I replied. "They are pretty sexy. Don't you think so?"

"They aren't human!"

Ah! Time to deliver the yorker. "Well... girls…human girls… don't have the sole right to be illogically logical. We guys can be like that too. And she…" I said patting my Triumph, "*is* a beautiful babe."

We had a logically illogical evening at Dilli Haat. With momos in Sikkim Stall and thepla with baingan ka chokha at another and super thanda coke. I had never come here before. Or perhaps… once. Anyway, I could have taken Apu to fifty different places with better food and ambience. But her illogical logic was that it would be a crime to coop ourselves inside four walls and a roof on such an evening. (I agreed with that). And as for ambience, nothing beat the colorful crowded chaos of Dilli Haat. (I didn't agree with that; never liked crowds too much, you should have some privacy with your date, and Dilli Haat was literally swarming that day!).

When we returned, Apu asked if I was in the mood for a walk. Of course I was, though I took care to hide my bubbling enthusiasm when I said yes. As we strolled towards the Mehrauli gate in the moon and street lamp lit night, Apu pointed to me the Director's house. "That's where the emperor lives."

I glanced at her. "Emperor?"

"Our Director."

I laughed. "You guys call your Director emperor?"

This was funny. I imagined *my* principal Dr. Wilson, with his large forehead, large specs and an equally large smile, decked as an emperor - crown and jewels and sword and all. Well... considering the volume of his head, he would perhaps need an extra large crown. And there would be chanting in Latin in our college halls and classrooms. *Ad Wilson Gloriam. To the glory of Dr. Wilson.*

Apu interrupted my flight of imagination. "No... *we* don't call him Emperor. I made it up right now. I thought it fits him... sort of..." she said shrugging.

"What's your Diro's name?" I asked.

"Prof. Sirohi."

"Emperor Sirohi?" I tried the moniker in a falsetto, as high as I could go.

"Hey! Keep it down!" she said alarmed. "You will have the guards on us!"

I ignored her and switched to vocal fry. She giggled involuntarily. A man going on a scooter turned his head and stared at us. Even the crows crowing nearby it seemed reduced their volume. *Stop now*, Apu pleaded.

Slowly, I shook my head. It was simply too much fun.

"Pleeeeassseeee!"

At last, I took pity on her and stopped. Then I told her the name wouldn't work. It didn't have enough…

"Ok!" Apu exclaimed. "I exaggerated! Lord have mercy on me!"

I grinned. "*When* don't you?" Though frankly, saying that to her was quite hypocritical considering my antics not seconds ago.

Apu glanced at me. "You felt that?" Her face sobered down and she let out a sigh. "Sorry. I didn't mean to. I guess it's become a habit."

Sorry?

Shit! You never know what hits a girl the wrong way, even IITians, especially illogically logical ones. I clutched her arm. "Hey! I didn't mean it like that. I actually like it… you being that way."

"You do?"

"Yup… And you are quite good at it," I said smiling at her. "One of the reasons I… you know… I got attracted and asked you out."

She brightened when I said that. Then looking up towards the sky where the clouds were hovering around the half moon, but not quite covering it, she said she got it from her mom. "Mom was quite witty. Much wittier. Dad says that's how he fell for her."

I thought I was listening to her. Yet somehow, I had missed the past tense and the wistfulness in her…

"Really? I would like to meet her."

She kept her eyes on the sky. "Mom is not..." There was a pregnant pause. "She was out fishing when she vanished into the sea. I was fourteen."

I cringed. "Oh! I am so-"

Apu interrupted. "It's cool. It's almost five years now, a long time." Then she stopped abruptly; I guess she didn't want to talk about the incident. Turning towards me, she smiled. "So what about your mom?"

"My mom? She's good."

"Aha…" Apu looked at me expectantly.

Was I expected to say something more? What?

Ok, let's do this. "Maa's very much alive," I said, jesting to change the mood. "I don't know if she quite believes in being witty. Religious. Aarti every evening. Leads us every year in competing for the *Hum Saath Saath Hain* award–"

Apu cut in again, eyes widened. "Are you joking?"

"Does it look like that?"

"You aren't happy with your mom?"

I told her it didn't even come to that. We didn't talk enough.

"Who doesn't talk enough? Your mom, or you?"

This was unbelievable! "Hey! You haven't even met her and you are taking her side!"

"I am not taking her side," Apu protested. "I am just saying… Look, your parents give you everything you want. You have the two choicest of bikes and sure a lot more. I am just guessing they care for you."

"Yes, they *certainly* care for me," I told her. For example, one could take my mom. She wanted me to wear ten rings on ten fingers. And would have wanted another ten for the toes! Unfortunately there were only *nine* planets...

They just didn't care for me in the way *I* wanted.

Apu smiled. "I guess we are in the same boat then. Thoda hai, thode ki jaroorat hai."

"No."

She frowned. "Huh?"

I explained. "Thode se *thoda kam* hai, thode se *thode jyada* ki jaroorat hai."

Apu grinned at those words. Then carefully clasping my fingers in hers, she asked archly: "Kya kam hai?"

Now *that* required a really long answer. Unfortunately, too many people were around us. The answer had to wait.

Delhi, 2003

Out below the clouds I rode, waving at the moon. On a black bike I rode, a dream that...

We were going to live that dream again. Soon. In a minute. The rain was beating down on us like crazy. The moon was a faint silhouette behind the clouds. You wouldn't look up and say it was a full moon day. I wanted to hear the wolves howl, the trees creak, the wind rustle through the leaves ominously. But we were in Delhi, so I had to be satisfied with the rain. Cold rain. Pouring rain. Shearing, scalding rain.

They say if you haven't ridden in the rain, you haven't ridden. They say it true.

I tightened my jacket and put on my fingerless leather gloves. Oh did they look good! Cool and mean. I took the last puff from the dying cigarette, threw it in the mud, and glanced at Rohan. He was already on his Harley. He nodded. The cue. We were ready to burn the wet road below and our souls above.

I mounted the Triumph Bonneville Rohan had got for me. Shit! I was riding history man! I was riding History! This was the mean machine Marlon Brando had swaggered upon in 'The Wild One', James Dean had sizzled on in 'The Rebel Without A Cause', and on which Bob Dylan had crashed himself and almost got killed. Many others from Hollywood had ridden it in more recent times, but I wouldn't take their names. They didn't match up.

Riding a Triumph required character, required angst. A spirit to rebel. Taste sweat and blood. At least sing mean anthems. Chocolaty spies wouldn't do.

We kicked. The machines roared. We waved at each other the Harley way. And the machine men were off.

A Harley Davidson and a Triumph Bonneville together should have turned heads. But who knew? - We were among illiterates.

Some of our friends even ask what's so big deal about a bike ride. What indeed? Bozos in cars. What would they know? They lived lives cooped up in a box. Insides fancy frames, metal or concrete. Their lives consisted of a few measly steps between different types of boxes. From a big box into a small one, back into a box again. Box, box and more boxes. And then a 7ft by 2 ft box in the end.

Their boxy lives wouldn't ever let them feel the moment. When all is one – the man, the machine, the moon, the rain, the road, the wind, the dull roar of the engine. And there is absolute silence. The silence of sound. Of rain, wind, moon and the night.

When the man is almost in love, part of something intense and beautiful. It's his night to live.

As Kundera wrote, *bent on his bike, he is here and now… NOW… rather he is outside time… in heavens… unaware of everything, his age, his wife, his children… everything. He is nothing, no one. Just a piece of unbelievable joy floating through space… like a Mozart symphony… without fear, because fear is in the future, and when there is no future, there is no fear.*

We were freed of fear, of the future. We were outside time. Outside worries, pain. They couldn't touch us through the wall of total, intense, beautiful silence. It was a gift of perfection from outside ourselves. The gift of a machine.

Hunched on our machines, on this night, we were Men, seeking, drinking, being that perfection.

Mumbai, Nov 27, 2008, 2:20 PM

Bodies were recovered by Naval commandoes. I didn't go to check this time. I couldn't.

Rohan told me Apu wasn't there.

Delhi, 2004

When I was twelve, I broke an expensive piece of glassware by flinging it against the floor. Nobody came to look.

They couldn't hear. Maa was busy in the kitchen, Dad with his papers in the office he had made for himself at home, Aaru I guess was sleeping. Anyway, she was too small. For nineteen days, I felt I was alone in the world till Gill Uncle came back.

Before going, he had given me a puzzle to solve. He called me in the afternoon, said, "Let's see if I can keep you busy for the next twenty days," and handed me the puzzle. A puzzle of numbers beautifully couched in a story of thieves and mangoes. I had to find the number of mangoes the thieves had. It was difficult, but I stayed up till early morning till mom forced me to sleep, then got back to thieves and mangoes as soon as I could.

Bleary eyed, when I finally solved it, I got why Gill Uncle had given me the puzzle. The answer was beautiful, elegant and simple. You just had to find the pattern, pick up the clues strewn on the road, and it led straight to the breathtaking answer. $\mathbf{x^{(x-1)}-1}$. Where 'x' was the number of thieves. That's it!

Journeys end in lovers meeting. I stared at the answer for a few minutes, marveling at its simplicity, and suddenly... I had to tell someone. I *had* to share! Tell how I had found it. Show how even the very difficult questions had sometimes breathtakingly simple answers. Just talk. My heart was bursting and I ran out of my room to find...

I came back soon. Maa said "Shaabash," complemented me for being intelligent, and refused to look at the puzzle saying the breakfast table had to be cleared and that I should better show it to dad. Dad refused to look saying he was busy and he might look at it later. Aaru was too small anyway.

That's when I came back and broke the glass. Nobody heard, so no big deal.

Since that day if I had to share something that made me really happy, I shared it with Gill Uncle. So one fine day, I told him about Apu.

"She's from Goa?" he asked while mixing his drink. It was his usual. Whiskey with soda and ice.

"Yup. And a Catholic," I added.

He turned towards me fully. "You aware what you're doing?"

"Very much."

"Really?"

"Why are you doubting me? It's nothing different from what you did."

"Me and Vani were from different states sir, not religion," he said.

"Would that have made any difference?"

He smiled from the bar. "Not really." Then he walked the few steps and sat down next to me. "Apu's the first girl you have told me about." His eyes twinkled. "I am guessing you are *deeply* in love with her?"

I swallowed. Was I deeply in love with Apu? Not really. But she did made me feel… different.

And I missed her. Regularly. Wasn't that enough?

"Isn't missing her regularly enough?"

For a couple of seconds he didn't reply. Then he turned his eyes to his glass and swirled the whiskey gently. "Look at the ice," he said. "Has it melted?"

A large crystal of ice floated in the whiskey. "No."

"Sticking out of the whiskey?"

"Yes."

He pulled out the ice crystal from the whiskey and put it on the table. "You need to *melt*," he said. "Otherwise, it will be easy to separate you two. Like this whiskey and ice. And god knows people will try." He smiled. "I guess you need to worry less. You are the pure ice… getting corrupted by the whiskey. You need to think about her. She will be branded the evil whiskey."

He put his glass on the table. "I suggest you melt in… or get out *now*."

I nodded. He was as clear as that crystal of ice.

Gill Uncle always was. A former World Bank economist, he was a famous person of our colony – apparently, he had played an important role in the 1992 economic liberalization, advising Manmohan Singh and all. Though when I asked him about it later, he dismissed it as a load of bunkum.

He came to live next door when I was quite small - just eight years old. A few months later, when I was almost nine, I flunked in a math exam having not seen any particular need to complete it. My worried parents, for whom the exam scores were reflection of math ability, took me to Gill Uncle to see if he could help me improve a bit.

"So you don't like maths?" he asked me as he pushed a plateful of dark chocolate balls towards me.

"It's boring," I told him while trying to chew three sizeable balls of chocolate at the same time. I quietly ignored my mother's furious waving that was meant to make me abstain.

"Boring!" he said shaking his head with laughter. He turned to my parents. "That's not the answer I expected."

He turned back to me. "Why do you find maths boring?"

I glanced at my parents trying to gauge their mood as a wrong answer could be risky. I had almost decided to hold my tongue when Gill Uncle made an offer I couldn't refuse. "Tell me the truth and you can have the whole bowl of chocolates," he said.

I looked at my parents again, but the temptation was too much. "The teacher makes us do the same thing again and again," I told him.

"And you would like to do different things every day?"

I nodded. I was beginning to like this guy.

I guess Gill Uncle felt the same way about me. He turned to my parents. "Ok, I will coach him and I am sure he will do better." My parents brightened. "But you will have to promise him one thing." He pointed in my direction.

"*Him*? What?" It was my dad. He was surprised. So was Ma, and so was I.

"You will have to let him have all the chocolates." He grinned at me.

That was my first lesson in motivation.

Delhi, 2004

I suddenly had a craving for those dark balls again. "Do you have my chocolates?"

He glanced at me with a mischievous twinkle. "Yes. And they are significantly improved."

I raised my eyebrows.

"Soaked in rum," he said grinning. Then he went and got me some. A couple of them, sinfully sweet, started melting in my mouth the next moment. I was happy, and in the mood for a love story - his and Vani's.

"So when did *you* melt?" I asked him.

He was mixing a second drink at the bar. "Give me a minute." He finished mixing his drink and walked over to the sofa. Then sitting down, he turned his head with a *cat ate all the cream* smile. "Guess?"

I did. Easily. There could be only one answer given his smile. "At first sight?"

He said it was a rainy day in 1967. College Street, Calcutta. The evening was cloudy. He was in the mood for coffee, as he was often in those college days. So his gumbal decided to go to a place that was known only to insiders - a small place away from the road, tucked in a corner behind a bookshop. It served the best cookies too.

He got up in the middle and went to the loo. While coming back, he had to walk between two tables kept really close, just enough to let one person through (it was a really small shop). Just as he entered that gap, a girl got up from the left table barring his way. She was still looking down, laughing, talking to her friend, her face clouded by her hair. She took a step like that, making him freeze. She was coming through too. He realized they would both have to squeeze through the gap as there was no other way. He sucked in his breath and moved.

Just then the lights went out.

He was in completely darkness. Squeezed against her awkwardly. Afraid to move, he could feel one of her legs pressed against his. He tried being a gentleman and pulled his leg back as much he could.

The lights wouldn't come back. Seconds went by. Almost a minute. And then perhaps it became too much for the girl too. She cleared her throat. Was that a signal? For what? Did she want him to say something? She cleared her throat again. Definitely a signal. What should he say? *What* should he say?

"Good evening," he said.

("What! You said *good evening*!"

"Shut up… and listen! I wasn't used to saying *hi*.")

"Good evening," the girl replied.

"It's really dark, isn't it?"

"Really dark."

"You came here for coffee?"

"No tea."

And then they ran out of conversation.

(You ran out of conversation! That was *conversation*!)

He was about to propose she ease back to her seat (how chivalrous!) when one of the waiters came in with a candle. Slowly there was enough light, he could see her outlines, but she didn't move. As if waiting for… *what*? To have a look at him? He was surprised… and pleased. He didn't move either. They both waited for the waiter to come close.

Then, in the light of the candle, he saw her eyes.

"And you melted?" I was incredulous.

"Yes."

"I don't believe you!"

"Your choice," he said shrugging and got up to get his third drink from the bar.

"I saw her photo. She's good, but –"

"Don't you dare!"

"Ok… ok."

I think I needed another chocolate. Or more rum.

This melting thing was crazy. Hell… difficult! I mean he just saw her eyes, *only eyes*, the first time. In comparison, I had seen Apu head to toe, or rather toe to head. And yet...

Would I melt? *Could* I melt? I wished I could. Whenever Gill Uncle talked about his happier times with Vani, his eyes were luminous, almost unearthly. Melting, definitely, seemed to be a *good* thing.

Perhaps he read my mind. "Have you told her?"

I looked at him. "Told her what?"

"You love her."

I said I didn't.

"But you miss her regularly."

That I did.

"Then how do you… Ok, I don't get this. You claim you miss Apu regularly. Yet you aren't in love with her. So can you please define love for me? What is it, in your *honorable* opinion?"

I sat thinking for a minute. What could I say? I tried escaping with the help of borrowed words. "Love is… love is a single soul inhabiting two bodies."

But he tripped me. He knew the line was borrowed. Crud!

"Don't quote Greek philosophers, especially those *dead for two thousand years*," he said. "Say something you feel."

Say something I feel? What did I feel? And why did it have to be original? Why couldn't I feel like a dead Greek philosopher? Dead Greek philosophers were good – they knew a lot about love. They ran around naked shouting like a madman, "Eureka, eureka… I have found it, I have found *it.*"

Wasn't that what love was supposed to be like? - *log kahen mujhe pagla kahin ka* and all.

"Love is… I don't know!"

"Then define it!" Gill Uncle said putting his glass on the bar with emphasis. "Let me help you if you can't. Define love as *missing her regularly.*"

"What! That's so arbitrary!"

"And you want love to be exactly what?"

I had no answer.

Delhi, 2004

So love, according to Gill Uncle was what we defined it to be. He had defined it for himself - as the *beginning*. He loved Vani, and that was the beginning of everything they had together.

Now it was my turn.

How should have I defined love? Was it missing Apu regularly? Wanting to hear her voice everyday? Thinking and laughing about her witty exaggerations even when I was alone? I didn't know.

So I called her up. It was almost midnight.

"Good evening," I said.

I could hear a yawn. She had been sleeping and I had woken her up. "*Good evening*!" she exclaimed. "Are you serious? It's twelve o' clock!" Then she paused. "What you been doing?"

"Good evening," I said again.

"Good evening. Are you drunk?"

"It's really dark, isn't it?"

She giggled. "Is it? Where are you?"

"In a place where I miss you."

She became silent.

"You know I want to hear your voice everyday. And I laugh at your jokes even when I am alone. Do you think I love you?"

No answer.

"Do you?"

"I think you should go to sleep," she whispered.

"So what? I will still see you in my dreams, and pester you there."

"You won't."

"How do you know?"

"I know," she said. "You will be in *my* dreams, not yours. There, I do all the bakbak and you just listen."

"Do I love you there?"

"I don't know. I haven't asked you yet."

"Ask me. Will you?"

I could hear her smile a slow, lovely smile. "Ok," she whispered.

I hung up, happy.

Delhi, 2004

"I think it's time you rebelled," Rohan told me.

He was talking about Apu and me, or more precisely, the places we went and things we consumed while on a date. Apu loved open places and thelawala food. While I was sort of ambivalent about them.

At first, I was dying to take her some place where a guy could suitably impress a girl. But after date after date of visiting IIT Canteen, Dilli Haat, Janpath and Kamala Nagar, I had recalibrated my expectations. Now I would have been happy to go any place they had four walls, a roof, a table and two chairs. If they had an AC, I would be happier. If they served cuisine other than Indian, you could perhaps find me dancing a jig.

"Why don't you tell that to Apu?" Rohan asked me uncomprehendingly.

"I don't know. It's difficult to explain. She seems happy when – "

"That's bullshit!" Rohan cut me off. "She's not going to become unhappy if you take her to some nice joint. Hey! That's what chicks are supposed to like."

Rohan said I was being a phattu. Worse, an *unnecessary* phattu! He could bet a thousand bucks Apu was going to like it if I took her to some good place.

I wasn't convinced. "How do I know where to take her?"

"Why? Just ask her… and be firm that it has to be some place where they serve champagne. It won't be a thela coz thelas don't serve champagne. May be in Vision 2050, but not yet."

I took Rohan's advice and told Apu while sitting in IIT canteen that next time we were going someplace they served champagne. Which meant IIT canteen, Dilli Haat, Janpath, Sarojini, Kamala et al were area non grata. She could choose any restaurant as long as it served champagne.

Apu was surprised. "What's the occasion?"

"None. I just want to take you to a nice place. Drink champagne. Make merry."

"You want to get me drunk!"

I stared at her. Gravely. Then made mean eyes, lowered my voice, and hissed: "Yesss! I am planning to date rape you."

Apu giggled. "You will have to pay for a lot of champagne before I get *that* drunk." She reached up and gently flicked a cowlick off my forehead. "And anyway you can't."

"*What do you mean I can't*?"

She giggled again. "Don't sweat. I am not insulting your manhood, no pun intended." She pinched my cheek. "You are just too cute for that."

Well… that was some comfort. Not that I wanted to rape anyone, but every male thinks he is an alpha male, and my alpha maleness had just been challenged. As was fated, it reared its head again when I arrived next time at Apu's hostel to take her out.

I had come to a screeching halt some 30 feet away. Yet, she didn't hear me come. She stood in front of her hostel, her back to me, laughing her head off with a handsome guy (I had to grudgingly admit that) with specs and curly hair. After examining him from head to toe, I discovered one fault with him – he wore hideous looking floaters. But that was little comfort, coz in spite of his poor taste in footwear, it didn't seem Apu would finish with him anytime soon. And the guy seemed to be funnier than Govinda – David Dhawan combo! Apu wouldn't stop laughing!

What were they laughing about so much? I felt I would soon be crying if I didn't stop them.

So I started strolling towards them. Totally nonchalant. My chest puffed up and my shoulder muscles flexed. Very casual. I wanted to make sure the curly haired nerd saw that I was about five inches taller than him. And much more muscular. And mean.

When I came within five feet of the pair, I said "hi", my voice as cool as possible. Both of them turned towards me.

Apu brightened when she saw it was I. The guy though, I *think*, went a shade paler.

"Hey!" Apu said, "Where were you? I was waiting for you."

Now was she? Didn't look like that. Then she gestured towards the chasmish. "This is Chinmoy. He is like... the quizwhiz of our class (quizzes in IIT lingo meant exams!). I was just telling him about you."

Thankfully, Chinmoy the quizwhiz boy (inwardly I was quite pleased that Chinmoy rhymed with *boy* and *not* with man), said bye to us not long after. My overpowering presence may have served as a strong incentive.

After he left, Apu told me he was called 'Cheeni' for short. And that the nickname fitted him - Chinmoy was a really 'sweet' guy. Sweet? Sweet as in what? - Sugar? Jaggery? Saccharine? I was a little unnerved by Apu's enthusiasm about Cheeni's sweetness, so I tried to move off him as the sweet topic.

"We need to decide where to go," I told Apu. "What's your favorite cuisine?"

Apu's lips curled with amusement. "Oh yes! I almost forgot. Are we are going to a champagne wala place today?"

I winced. Champagne *wala* place! "Yes."

"Do I have to wear an evening gown and all?" she ribbed me.

"No, my lady," I ribbed her back getting on the bike. "Jeans and top and large ear rings will do. Now what do you want to *eat*?"

"Anything," she said.

"Define anything."

She replied anything meant anything. I allowed that being a she-human of the Indian variety, I was sure she didn't actually mean *anything* when she said anything. For example -

She cut me off. "Before you say something really gross… what choices do I have?"

I smiled with satisfaction, and reeled off a few names... "Indian, Chinese, Italian, French, Mexican, Thai…"

She said all of them were good with her. All of them were good with me too, so I said why didn't we roll a dice to make a choice.

"But I don't have a dice!"

"I have," I replied taking out one from my jacket pocket.

"Wow! That's resourceful!"

I took a mock bow. "Always at your service madam."

Then her eyes narrowed. "Do you gamble mister?"

"No," I said sweetly. "Knowing you, I anticipated that we may have to roll a dice to…"

She made a face, snatched the dice from my hand, and chucked it back at my face. "Get to work you smartass." I caught the dice in time before it hit my nose.

I threw the dice and it threw back at us the number six. We had decided number six would be Thai, so I expressed my satisfaction with the outcome by yodeling loudly. "Yoohoo!"

It was not the smartest of moves. Apu looked at me doubtfully. "What's your favorite cuisine?"

"Why?"

"Just asking."

I confessed that my favorite cuisine was Thai. But that was just a coincidence.

Apu refused to believe me. *I knew it,* she said tossing her head with phony anger. "I won't go to eat Thai. I have been cheated. The dice is loaded."

"Hello! It's not!"

"It is!" Apu put her hand on her breast. "How could have I been so naïve?"

Apparently, she was the poor village girl. (*Village girl! In top and jeans and large earrings?).* Going out with me, a suave urban economist. And as everyone knew, economists could never play fair.

Was this a plan to guilt trip me out of eating Thai? If so, it wasn't going to work. "Nice try," I retorted. "The dice is *not* loaded." No modern village girl was going to con me; I had won the toss free and fair. And talking about fairness, I told her I was not the one flirting with sweet Cheeni.

Apu's eyes widened. "Are you serious?"

"What does it look like?" I replied, only half-joking.

"Ohmigod! You are jealous!" she exclaimed.

Oops! This was bad. I had not planned on my secret getting out. So I protested that of course I was only joking. Cheeni couldn't flirt if his life depended on it - he was an IITian.

That got to Apu. "Hello! I am an IITian too!"

"So who said you could flirt?"

Apu shook her head with disbelief. Saying I deserved to be punished for insulting her and her college… "and my dear friend Cheeni," she added… she informed me that she had changed her mind. This evening, she would eat only Chinese cuisine coz that was her favorite.

"But five minutes back you said you had no favorites!"

"I changed my mind. I am a complicated woman."

"That's not fair!"

"Do you want Cheeni to take me out then? Cheeni likes Chinese."

Of course, what *else* would Cheeni like? Aaaaaaaaaaa.........

It was thus that the Chinese won over the Thai in the battle of the cuisines. Helped by a complicated woman who had cheated in their favor and who now sat behind me on the bike, her arms around me, singing loudly: "Sugar sugar... cheeni cheeni... you're my candy guy and you got me wanting you..."

I sincerely hoped I was the guy she was singing about. Forget alpha male... I was even ready to be a *candy guy* now. Goddamned Cheeni!

Mumbai,

In the nearby Golden Dragon Chinese restaurant, cutlery filled with half-finished food lay spread across the room on sauce stained table cloths. Bullet marks and shrapnel from grenades filled the walls - the result of a long battle between the attackers and defenders.

The fight had almost destroyed the restaurant's captivating picture window, turning it into shards of glass. Worse, fire had scorched parts of Golden Dragon and now pools of detritus filled water lay here and there, the evidence of the efforts of those who had bravely extinguished the fire.

Delhi, 2004

Rohan was right. Champagne wala place funda had worked. Apu was absolutely gorging on the Duck dimsums we had ordered at House of Ming, one of my favorite Chinese restaurants. "This is yum..mmy," she exclaimed putting one of them in her mouth.

I gave her a *I told you so* look. Then to drive home the point I added loftily: "Have you ever tasted better dimsums?"

"Yup, I have," Apu replied.

"Really? When?"

"When it was made by yours truly."

I was surprised. "Liar!"

"I am not lying," she said.

I said "nice try", so she persisted: "Sacchhi! God promise! I can make very good dimsums. As good as these. I learnt from my dad."

Apu had told me her dad Jerry ran a restaurant near Vagator beach in Goa and was a fabulous cook, so the claim could be true. "You can cook Chinese?"

"I can cook pretty much everything." She couldn't hide the pride in her voice. "I grew up helping mom and dad."

Well… I was floored. That was a really big achievement by my standards.

If anything, I wasn't born to cook. The last time I tried to make an omelet, I got egg over my face literally - my nose, my ear, my shoulder, my t-shirt… I will never forget the pitiful look in our cook's eyes who was thankfully the sole witness to the event. I may have learnt economic fundas with ease, but ande ka funda? – I had no clue!

"Wow! Aren't you the dream girl for foodies!" I teased her. "Falling in love with you would be rewarding."

"What if it's not?" Apu asked suddenly, gazing into my eyes.

The words stunned me. And the abrupt change in the tone of her voice. Why had she said that? What was she thinking?

"Yes…" I asked hesitatingly. "You don't think so?"

She leaned back a little. "I don't know Ani. I feel… scared."

"Scared… *What happened*?"

She let her head roll back so she was looking up at the ceiling. "I don't know... I... Because we are so different. Almost from different worlds."

... ...

"I can't even think of..." She straightened and brought her eyes back on me. "I can't even *think* of ordering a 9000 bucks Pinot Noir," she said referring to the champagne. "That's the money I live on for 3 whole months."

Just as I had feared - the rich guy-poor girl...

"How does that say we are different Apu?" I cried, half tempted to give the girl a knock on her head. "I am just a little richer, that's all!"

She smiled a wan smile. "A little?"

"Yes. A *little*!" I said. "Can't a guy try to impress a girl once in a while? I don't order champagne everyday!"

I reminded her that she had dragged me along to all the thelawala places she liked and I hadn't said a word. Today for once I got her to a champagnewala place and she... It was not fair!

She didn't reply immediately. Picking up the fork, she grazed a pointed end on the tablecloth for a while. Then she looked up into my eyes. "I am sorry Ani. I am scared because I... I like you."

Yet we were from *such* different worlds. What if?

I started cursing Rohan. And the champagne bottle. And House of Ming. Wish I hadn't listened to the idiot! Dilli Haat was good. Parothas in IIT Canteen were even better. And nothing beat *nothing*. Next time I would go to meet Apu on a Bajaj scooter. Or on cycle. Or on foot. When I came back to this world, Apu was saying something about us being from different reli...

No! I cut her off, reached out and clutched her hand. "Apu please! Let's not talk about those things. They don't matter! You know I love you!"

"You do?" she said half smiling.

"Yes."

"You never said it before."

"I didn't?"

She nodded her head from side to side.

"Ok… then I will say it now." I clutched her hand tightly. "I love you, I love you, I love you. Three times. I love you, I love you. Five times. I love you, I…

"I love you too."

"I love you three."

Apu's smile widened. "I love you four." She was back in the game! – I was so relieved. And before I could open my mouth, I was firmly told not to say a word more.

"Why?" There I had said my one word.

"Because I am Aparajita… remember?" she said. "The unbeatable. You can't love me five," she said giggling.

"Applies to love too?"

"Darling, that applies everywhere."

I didn't mind. As long as I was her darling. We were awesomely dimsumly happy.

Mumbai, Nov 27, 2008, 12:33 PM

"The battery will… it will die anytime Ani," she said sobbing. "I won't be able to talk. I… I am scared. I want to talk to you. I don't want to die. Dibbs didn't do anything to anybody. Then why?" she broke down.

"Nothing will happen to you baby… *nothing*. I promise." I promised. I lied. The impotent husband.

"Yes, nothing will happen. I will *not* die." She sobbed once. "I am switching my cell off Ani. Then I… I can at least SMS from time to time. Ok. Will I?"

"Yes, baby." There was no other way.

"Ok."

"But SMS every five minutes."

"Ok."

There was a pause.

"I want to hold you Ani."

"Me too baby."

"Tight. Once even if I die."

"*Don't*," I bellowed.

Pause again.

"Where's daddy?"

"Next to me. I will give the phone to him."

They talked for a minute. Then Jerry gave the phone back to me.

"Hey!" I said.

"I love you," said Apu.

"I love you too."

"I lo… Bye Ani." Beep beep.

She didn't complete it. She didn't win this time. There was no time.

Delhi, 2004

"Say I love you," I demanded from Apu. It was late evening, about ten, and we were chatting on the phone. I am from my cell phone, she from the landline in her hostel lobby.

"I can't."

"Why not? Is Cheeni there?"

"Ha ha ha… very funny."

"Then?"

"Cheeni isn't there, but my warden *is* there."

Apu's warden was Prof. McGonagall Gokhale from the Electrical Engineering department. She was called McGonagall because in IITD junta's opinion, she resembled Prof. McGonagall from the Harry Potter movies. Supposedly a terror to the electrical engineering students for her liberal distribution of fakkas (the fail grade for the IIT population) in her Control Systems course, Prof. McGonagall was equally generous in spreading terror in Kailash Hostel whenever an opportunity presented itself. Apparently, this was a good opportunity to terrorize Apu.

"Be brave." I tried to pump Apu up. "Pyar kiya toh darna kya. Parda nahin jab koi khuda se, *warden* se parda karna kya."

It didn't work. "Shut up!" I was told. "It's not the time to joke!"

"Why are you whispering?"

"Because she is staring at me with her owlish eyes!"

Apu was especially afraid of Prof. McGonagall's owlish eyes because her equally owlish ears had somehow managed to hear that Apu had returned with me beyond the curfew time quite a few times, and she had called Apu and given her a sound dressing down for returning too late to hostel. It had been a real dampener as it had led to us cutting down significantly on the time we could spend together.

But we accepted the change philosophically. Yeh duniya wale toh *always* poochenge.

"Hello! Where are you?"

"What?" she said.

"Why are you *silent*?"

"Because I am grinning my entire battisi at the bitch!" she exclaimed. "Hey! I will talk to you later," she said. "She will keep hounding me if I stay. Bye."

"No! Wait…" But Apu had cut the phone.

That pissed me off majorly. Tonight I had definitely overshot my quota of sweet nothings without getting even one I ♥ U from Apu. All because of Prof. McGonagall!

I wished I knew some curse like Disappeario Totalis to make the revered professor disappear *totally* from our lives. Unfortunately, that wasn't possible; I was as Muggle as they came.

Then I had second thoughts about the matter. Granted the awful Prof. McGonagall did her very best to be the kabab mein haddi in our love affair. But so would have my mom if I gave her a chance. I don't think maa would have left me in *heavenly peace* if she heard me blowing kisses or mouthing I ♥ U to Apu over the phone.

But she never *could* become the haddi because I never gave her a chance. I never gave her a chance because I never called Apu from our landline. And I never called Apu from our landline because I had a cell phone!

Bingo! Chacha Chaudhary ke dimag ki batti jal gayi re! - Apu needed a cell phone. Then from the privacy of her room no. 322, she could say as many I ♥ Us to me as I wanted.

Yes! Now I would make her make up for all the I ♥Us I had missed till date. And Prof. McGonagall would be able to do nothing, her owlish eyes and ears notwithstanding. McGonagall Ali… pyar ki dushman hai hai… pyar ki dushman meri jaan ki dushman hai hai…

The next time I called her, I told Apu she should get a cell. Then no McGonagall will ever come between the two of us.

I was expecting her to appreciate the fantastic brainwave that would solve our problems in a chutki. But all she said was a "Hmm…"

"What hmm…?" I asked, a little offended at the cool reception.

"Aren't you forgetting something sweety?"

"Forgetting?"

"Mr. Richie Rich!" she said. "A cell phone costs a few thousand bucks (those were the early days and the mobile revolution hadn't happened yet). Where would I get it? Last I knew, the Indian Govt. wasn't allowing Aparajita Pinto to mint money!"

I didn't argue with her. I just said ok. I had plans of my own. It was time Miss Aparajita Pinto got a surprise.

When we met next Friday evening, I told Apu that either I would give her a cell phone as a gift so she could speak to me privately, or she had to promise to say I ♥U to me, McGonagall or no McGonagall. So what was it going to be?

She didn't answer my question. Instead, she said: "If you don't want to meet me anymore, say that straight."

"Huh?"

"McGonagall is going to put me in room arrest if I say I ♥ U before her! And then who would rescue me… the damsel in distress from the dragon!" she said pouting.

As if that would cut ice with me. "Bull!" I replied - if she was ever the damsel, it was not her but the *dragon in distress* that would need to be rescued from her. Anyway, since she wasn't brave enough to confess her love for me before McGonagall (how unromantic), she could always choose the other option of let her stinking rich boyfriend buy her a cell phone. But the I♥ Us were non-negotiable.

"I can't do that Ani," she said scratching the edge of the cup of cappuccino before her. We were sitting in a coffee joint close to JNU.

"Why?"

"I don't know! I just can't."

I was vexed. This was like being irrational. "What's the big deal? It's just a small gift!"

"It's not small Ani! If it was small, I wouldn't…"

"It *is* small! I give a gift like this to Aaru every other month!"

"She's your sister!"

"You're my girl!"

"There's a difference."

"What difference? I love her. I love you… It's my right!"

"Ani stop it!"

I stopped, furious.

I was hurt. Couldn't she accept from me a small gift? Were we so far apart? Then why claim to love each other? Was there any difference between a stranger and me? Why didn't she simply…

"I am sorry Ani," Apu said gazing into my eyes. Her face was sad.

But I wasn't appeased. I told her I hadn't committed a crime by being rich. That I was aware of *that* difference between us every day. Scared every moment if I would do anything that would bring it up.

Then, suddenly aware that people were looking at us, I lowered my voice to a biting whisper. "*Why* is it such a big deal?"

She didn't say a word for a while. Then she looked away. When I saw her eyes again, two small droplets were shining at the corners. "Because I promised my mom," she said.

I quietly raised my eyebrows. I was feeling a little guilty for shouting at her.

She told me it was the year her mom died. On Valentine's Day, a rich guy from the neighborhood who had a crush on her had given her an expensive perfume. Her mom found that out by chance and tore into her. She had seldom seen her mom so angry.

"Mom told me I was too young for such things, and anyway you didn't accept gifts so expensive that you couldn't give back something similar when time came. She made me promise I wouldn't do anything like that again."

"But you were too young then. And you didn't love the guy."

"I know. But I promised her. And I…" she caught her throat. Then recovered. "I never had the chance to ask her again."

I gripped her hand and squeezed it gently. There was nothing more to say really.

She smiled after a long time. At least it seemed so. "Hey! I didn't say thank you to you."

"For what?"

"For trying so hard to give me a gift." She grinned.

I grinned back. "The motive was purely selfish. You don't have to."

I took out the silver colored Motorola cell phone I had brought for her. It was a model one of my dad's friend imported from god knows where. "I think my sister is going to have a third cell phone soon."

"You already bought the phone?"

"Yes. I thought I would surprise you."

Apu gazed into my eyes for a few seconds in a way I couldn't make out. "What are you thinking?" I asked her.

She shook her head, then covered her face with her hands. After a while, I saw her face again. She was smiling. "Give it to me."

I was happily surprised. "Really?" I pushed the phone towards her.

"Yes," she said slowly. "I was talking to my mom." She closed her eyes, then opened them again. "Said I was sorry, but had to break my promise. This time it was… different. She said it was ok… I think."

I smiled. "Your mom approves of me?"

Apu smiled back. "I think… yes. But don't try giving me another phone when I lose this one. That would definitely piss her off."

That got me coughing. "What! *When* you lose this one?"

"Yep!" Apu replied grinning impishly. "Who knows what the future may bring?"

My hands itched to wring her neck.

Well, the future didn't actually bring the loss of a Motorola cell phone belonging to a certain Miss Apu Pinto. But in spite of its silvery sleeky presence, it was not of much use to her. And me. The damn girl forgot to charge it regularly. The last time I tried arguing with her to please remember charging her cell, I was sweetly told that wasn't *her forgetting to charge her cell*, a blessing in disguise?

I was foxed. "Blessing in disguise?"

"Yes," my sweetheart explained to me. "See that's an excuse for us to meet and say *I love you* face to face."

I gave up.

Mumbai, 2008

Who knows what the future may bring?

About 10 pm on the night of Nov 26, two terrorists attacked Leopold Cafe, spraying bullets onto the people inside before fleeing. 10 people were killed and many were injured, including a news reporter. After Leopold, the attackers took a lane which lead to the prestigious Taj Hotel just a few meters away. The assailants entered the ground floor area and started firing indiscriminately.

Delhi, 2004

Aparajita Pinto ko gussa kyon aata hai?

Jab Aniruddh Hirani breaks a bone in drag racing. Radial bone of the left arm to be precise. It was nothing much really, just a hairline fracture, yet Apu's wrath struck me like Indra's lightening bolt.

Rohan was the chief culprit behind this incident because of which Apu refused to see my face. If he hadn't invited that moron Dikki to a weekend party we were having at his home, none of this would have happened.

The dude was called Dikki for a very funny reason. Apparantly, the dude was doing some chick, of all places, in his garage. Then his dad arrived quite unexpectedly, and Dikki had to ask the chick, who like him was in her birthday suit, to get inside the dikki (bonnet) of the car. When Dikki hastily dressed up and opened the garage shutter, it turned out dad dear had come to take one of the spare cars as his own Mercedes' engine had conked. The rest, as they say, was history.

The story was spread out by dad's driver, and since then Dikki - whose actual name was Nilesh Pujara - was called by everyone Dikki. Of course behind his back; he blew his fuse if anyone said that name to his face.

I had never liked Dikki. He had never anything to talk about besides which chick he had most recently conned into sleeping with him (I had the suspicion at least 90% of his stories were made up; otherwise he would soon surpass Genghis Khan in the number of women he had done). Unfortunately, Dikki had picked up bike racing as another hobby in recent times, and according to reports, had become pretty good at it. That's why Rohan had softened towards him and invited him to the party.

Bad decision. We were halfway through the party and I was taking my rare tequila shots when Dikki decided to renew a non-existent friendship.

"Hey dude. Wassup?" he greeted me.

"Doing good dude. You?" Tequila had made me light hearted and I could happily entertain even Dikki.

"Don't ask man. Shitty stuff happening. You remember that chick from…"

Time to leave my body and roam around till Dikki finished with the tale of his latest chick. When I returned Dikki was asking me why wasn't I seen around these days.

"Nothing much dude. Generally busy."

"Really? I heard you got a girlfriend."

I stiffened. Dikki was the last person in the world I would have wanted to talk to about Apu.

I shrugged. "Nothing serious." I had doubts he would understand *seriousness* anyway. Then to divert his attention from Apu, I brought up another topic guessing it would be one of his favorites now. "I heard you became a Bond at drags."

I was right. His face lighted up from ear to ear. But with a feigned humility that broadcasted *ah! Even you know about it!* he replied, "Nothing grrreat man." He had a funny way of rolling his "R"s as if he had spent his entire childhood in Washington DC (he hadn't). "Just some practice. Couldn't beat Rohan or you. You guys are the Bonds."

"Rohan maybe. Not me."

"Sure man. Rohan's the best. But you are great too. What about showing me your stuff once?" he said displaying his teeth.

I got what he was hinting at. He wanted to race with me and show off to others that he could beat me. "I don't do drags," I said.

"Come on man. I heard you beat so many guys. I was even there once when you beat that… some Nischal dude from Hansraj."

Shit! Was this guy following me or what! I knew he could be a real pain in the ass if he chipkoed to you. I tried to fob him off. "Dude… that was more than a year ago. I don't do drags anymore!"

He smiled dirty. "Why? Girlfriend doesn't allow?"

Let me tell you why I agreed to race Dikki - I was an idiot! Once he brought Apu into the conversation, I became afraid that if I refused him, I would be branded a wimp in our circle. Our dislike was mutual, and asshole that he was, I thought it would not take him long to spread that I was afraid of my girlfriend and had given up drag racing at her command. The alpha male in me couldn't take that.

We decided to fix the race for the following Friday night. Manesar Road – we were told thullas had started patrolling Delhi-Noida toll road, so we had to strike out our first option. A guy named Chacko, another good racer, agreed to do the honors of being the 'Starter' and flagging us.

By the time I reached the venue on Friday night along with Rohan (I had lied to Apu that I was busy studying), a small group of racing enthusiasts had already gathered there. I was mildly famous among the biking fraternity having won many bets and was rumored to have even done a 'goose eggs' once (which was false of course). Also, a few more bets had been added onto the bet between Dikki and me. More than five races would happen today.

I greeted a few of the bikers whom I knew. They said they were glad to see me back on the circuit. Then I heard girls screaming. Turning to find out what was going on, I saw Dikki had arrived and started showing off already. Big surprise. He was doing wheelies, which I was told he had learnt recently, to the lusty cheers of a couple of chicks.

Huh… Dikki! I just wanted to finish the race quickly and get back.

To be honest, I was pretty unsure about winning. I was totally out of practice and you don't win these things without a lot of practice.

Even Dikki knew that. When we lined up, the bastard went deep stage, played tricks, and I realized he was trying to get me to foul – that is make a start before Chacko had flagged us. That would have got me disqualified.

Nice try dude! I held my cool in the burndown. Bloody ass didn't know I was never a pushover.

But I was destined to lose, out of touch that I was for a whole year. As I had feared, I royally screwed up on my reaction time – the time to get myself moving once we were given the green signal. The distance we would race was only about quarter of a mile, and with our speeds, the race would be over in less than ten seconds. With my late reaction, no amount of gain on E.T, the actual racing time, could have helped me.

Before a second was over, I was beaten.

But if you are in a race, you race, whether you win or not. I went after Dikki, determined to salvage my honor.

As a general rule, drag racing is done on a straight track. But because policemen were after us and beggars can't be choosers, this time it was different. In the stretch of the road we were forced to choose for the race, there was a slight bend in the road about three-quarters of the distance.

Dikki was racing about twenty meters ahead of me. Just as he took the bend, he skidded without reason. Tumbling off the bike, he went rolling down the road as if a football kicked by Beckham. His bike went screeching and somersaulting up the road throwing sparks like a spinning wheel during Diwali.

That's when I skidded too.

But I was lucky. Dikki's accident had given me just the split half-second to realize there was something unknown on the road that had caused Dikki to tumble off his bike. I would most likely suffer the same fate.

I was fortunate in one more way. Today, I had come prepared for any accident. I guess I had become more careful about such things since I fell for Apu. Perhaps that is also a part of love - being careful about your life because someone you care for cares for it. I had fortressed myself in a leather jacket with heavy padding on the spine, shoulders, elbows and wrists, leather gloves with knuckle protection, boots, and a full face helmet.

They saved me. I tumbled off my bike and rolled like Dikki, but I didn't hurt myself bad like him. That he had unluckily crashed into a tree in the end made his injuries worse – he ended up breaking his nose, his wrist and an ankle. He also dislocated his hips and concussed his head. I in contrast escaped with just a hairline fracture to my left radius.

Both of our bikes skidded and somersaulted off the road into the grass. Fortunately, mine didn't crash into his. Otherwise they could have caught fire and got us in deeper shit!

When I got up, ran to the criminal spot and investigated, I found scores of wet leaves spread over the area. No idea where they had come from since the nearest tree – the one in which Dikki had unluckily crashed - was about thirty feet away. Perhaps they had been dropped by some vehicle.

It was difficult to understand how the guys who had checked the track for basic safety had failed to notice them. More likely, the guys simply didn't know wet leaves could be dangerous!

I swore. I should have checked the track myself.

Then I ran to help Dikki who to my panic wasn't getting up. That was an indication things were real bad with him. When I got to him, he was groaning with pain but conscious. I was relieved. He may have to spend a lot of time in the hospital, but he would live to impress and do more chicks. That was good enough for me.

The people standing at the finis line had begin to reach us by that time. Soon Dikki was lifted into a car and rushed to the hospital. I refused to accompany the lot. I told them I was ok enough – I mean my arm was hurting, quite a bit, but the pain was bearable. We strapped my bike on top of SUV of Daljeet, a friend of ours, and left the scene.

Delhi, 2004

I crashed that night at Rohan's place to avoid the piercing eyes of my family. The next day the doctor Ms. Mishra told me that I had a hairline fracture. "You will need a cast for five to six weeks to heal the fracture completely."

I grimaced.

"If you don't take good care of the arm, you can break the same place clean. You want that?" she said.

My grimace disappeared. Hairline fracture was bad enough. I didn't want to break *anything* clean.

For my family, I made up the story that I had hurt myself playing basketball. Both maa and Aaru gave me an earful for not being cautious. And I think Aaru, who knew I raced, didn't quite believe me either.

Then there was the matter of Apu.

And the matter had become knotty. Totally uljha hua. It was difficult to make her swallow the cock and ball story I had made up for my family. She had called me yesterday late night around eleven when I was at Daljeet's house readying myself for the race and I had sworn to her that I was doing *nothing* but studying. Curlty conscious, I even volunteered to read out to her what I was studying – a profit and loss statement from one of Daljeet's books. Luckily Apu had no idea accounting was not a part of economics.

Being caught by her while fibbing, I decided, would be much worse than telling the truth. So I told her the truth.

I may not have done that if I knew she would get so hopping mad. "I am NOT going to love a guy who will kill himself anyway!" she yelled at me and cut the phone.

She wouldn't pick up my calls after that. So I called her from Rohan's phone. She listen to my pleadings quietly, but refused to meet me. Undeterred, I went to see her unannounced. In an auto. Both firsts for me.

For a while it seemed even that would be futile. She didn't come down to the lobby. Then just when I was leaving, I saw her entering the lobby door.

Before I could say a word, she gestured me to shush. She examined my cast carefully. After satisfying herself that things were fine, she turned to me. "Now say what you have to say," she said imperiously.

"You know I have every intention of strangling you!"

"You can't do that." She was all disdain. "You don't even have a left hand."

Is it fair to hold one responsible if that makes you want to utter your entire collection of choice swear words?

"I *have* a left hand Apu!" I howled. "It's just broken a *little*!"

"Big difference."

"Why the hell are you *so* angry? I have not killed myself, have I?"

She sighed. "Yes. That's exactly the day I should wait for. *And home they brought the biker dead.*"

Well… that made me a little sheepish. Her words had hit home. Especially when you considered what had happened to Dikki yesterday. But I was not about to show that. It would be disastrous.

"Don't exaggerate khali-peeli!" I said instead.

"I am not exaggerating!" Apu snapped. She asked if I had any idea of the death rates in bike racing. "It is the fourth most dangerous sport in the world. Even more dangerous than bull fighting!"

Trust her to do the IITian thing. "Don't throw stats at me Apu," I said slightly pissed. "I know about the dangers. I have lived and breathed the sport since I was fifteen."

"So it was not an accident then. You were trying to commit suicide."

Now I was really pissed. "Are you done?"

"No! I am not done!"

"Then go to hell!"

"Maybe I will. To my room."

"Fine."

"Fine."

I stomped off from Kailash Hostel.

Before I had gone a kilometer, I was repenting my decision. I got down from the auto at a roadside shoppee to have a much needed smoke. Calmed, I stood there for some time thinking. Thinking was the wrong solution. Soon I began feeling bad. Worse. Horrible. I shouldn't have told her to go to hell. That was mighty rude. She was just angry because she was scared for me. Aaaaaaaahhhhhhh…

For two whole days I wished she would melt and call me. That didn't happen, in spite of staring ten times at my cell every waking hour. Alternating between anger and pain, there were occasions when I almost picked up the phone to say "sorry", but…

I didn't get any brilliant idea even the third day, so I decided to take the help of Gill Uncle to engineer a truce. Of course, without telling him the entire story.

"Why don't you call Apu for dinner tomorrow?" I suggested to him as we played chess in the evening. He was winning handsomely, so it seemed a good time.

"Should I? Is it her birthday?" He was excited.

"No, it's not her birthday. You know… ainwaiee."

"Ainwaiee?" He looked at me quizzically.

I nodded.

"But why you want to waste a date with your girl on an old man?"

I grinned. "Ainwaiee."

"Ok." He grinned back with a shrug. "Anyway, great for me. I will get to see her at last. Tell her that Uncle Gill has invited her for a lavish dinner day after tomorrow."

"Why not tomorrow?"

"What's so special with tomorrow?" he asked. "I need time to receive the young lady. At least a couple of days."

Young lady? He sounded like an English Lord or something. And why he needed two days to call her? Were we having a royal banquet with the Queen of England?

I just needed Apu here! Fast! How could I explain that to him?

Anyway, I let it go. If I could bear three painful days… ek aur sahi.

Delhi, 2004

I had never seen Gill Uncle misty-eyed before. Forget misty-eyed, I hadn't even seen him sad before. Even when he mentioned his dead wife and daughter, which was rare, he did it almost matter of factly. I knew he had loved his wife Vani intensely, and his daughter too, though she was very small when the car carrying her and Vani tumbled off a mountain road in Bolivia where they had gone for a holiday. That's why I admired him for the way he managed to hold his emotions back even when reminded of a tragedy of such scale – as it must be whenever he mentioned his wife or daughter.

But today, for the first time, I saw small tears shining at the corners of his eyes. Apu was the reason. He said she reminded him of Durga, the daughter he had lost when she was only two.

"I think if she had grown up, Durga would look just like you," he told Apu, kissing her on her forehead. I was touched. I think so was Apu.

Then he got something from the nearby closet. It was similar to one of those velvety red rectangular boxes in which my mom kept her… *gold ornaments*! He opened it. It contained what looked like an expensive white gold necklace. Apu glanced in my direction.

Coincidentally that's when I was smitten by a pair of gray wooden elephants placed at the opposite end of the room - I couldn't take my eyes off them. My ears, however, were focused on what would happen between the 'old man' and the 'young lady'. It should be interesting considering this was the same young lady who had made me sweat buckets when I tried to give her a paltry cell phone.

But what followed was an anti-climax: the young lady surrendered meekly. Taking the necklace from the old man, she wore it then and there. I shouldn't be saying this perhaps, but I actually felt cheated. I was expecting a high voltage melodrama.

"It looks so pretty on you," Gill Uncle told Apu. "Doesn't it Aniruddh?" he involved me.

"Ya… it does!" I said, nodding as much as the structural mechanics of my head permitted. I was desperate to get into the good books of my girl.

We had a lavish dinner – a mix of Indian and Italian cuisine. Soup and light pasta followed by rumali roti, pulao and mutton do pyaja, followed by chocolate truffles and blueberry cheesecake. After dinner we occupied the sofas for a chat session. I had high hopes resting on it. Surely Gill Uncle would work his magic with Apu.

He started the conversation with Apu on an inquisitive note. "So does he behave like the suitable boy to you?" he asked her.

Apu frowned for a second, perhaps trying to get the meaning of the question. Then she said: "Yes, most of the times."

"Most? Give me an exact figure. You must be good at maths."

I could have sworn Gill Uncle winked at Apu as he said that.

"Why are you winking?"

"Winking? Who's winking? I am not winking!"

Liar!

Apu grinned. She was beginning to understand this. Looking up as if calculating deeply she said, "Umm… about 83%," she bit her lip.

83%? From where the hell had she arrived at a figure like *that*?

"And the rest 17%?" Gill Uncle winked again.

I sighed. Et tu Uncle Gill?

"Unsuitable…" Apu sighed too. "I guess nobody's perfect."

"True… not even Aniruddh Hirani. Though I am not sure *he* knows he's not perfect," Gill Uncle said. He was nodding as if they had arrived at an *eternal* truth after years of chintan baithak. "What's he done recently?"

Apu bit her lips again. "Went racing. I guess he wanted to kill himself, but didn't succeed. Just broke his arm and came back."

Gill Uncle looked at me, surprised. "I didn't know this. You know he lied to me and everyone else that he broke it playing basketball!"

Apu was surprised too. "Really?"

"Yes! The 6ft 1inch chicken!"

Apu glanced in my direction. (I saw that with the corner of my eye). But I was already looking the other way, deeply engrossed in the beauty of the tusky, dusky elephants. Ok, fine, I was a 6ft 1 inch chicken. But so was she before her warden, isn't it? God the lies she had made up for McGonagall to explain her late returns to hostel!

"So should we punish him for this?" Uncle asked Apu. "Kya kiya jaaye? Maar diya jaye... ya chhor diya jaye?"

By now, Apu had failed in her attempts to curb a smile and was grinning widely. She glanced at me once more. This was our first big fight. I mean the kind of fights where you refuse to talk to each other for days because of your ego and keep smoldering inside. Uselessly. I wanted it to end. I made a contrite face and waited.

I guess Apu wanted the same. "Chhor diya jaye."

Yesss!

But if I thought my ragging at the hands of the two conspirators was over, I was mistaken. Gill Uncle was not satisfied taking my case yet. "What are you asking him in return?" he asked Apu.

She frowned. "In return?"

"Yep. No plans to ask the dude anything in return? Len-den? Dena-paona? Quid pro quo? I give you this, you gimme that?"

"Oh yes!" Apu's eyes brightened. "I totally forgot." She looked up tapping her chin for half a minute as if she was Newton contemplating the fall of the apple on her head. Drama Queen! "What should I ask him?"

"Tell him to lay off racing so he doesn't kill himself someday, and then lie to Yamaraja that he killed himself playing *basketball*."

"No!"

Gill Uncle smiled at me sweetly. "Mr. Racer, it's the lady who decides. Of course if you don't want Apu to forgive you…" He left the sentence hanging.

I never knew he could be such a devil. This was a like… a perfect *set-up*!

However, I had hopes for the future. When I looked at Apu, she was grinning from ear to ear. She was happy. A happy Apu was a generous Apu. And the generous Apu had forgiven me. For now that was enough.

Racing could wait.

Mumbai, Nov 27, 2008, 5:19 AM

Dibbs had died very quickly. Within two minutes of being shot. Apu said she was not able to speak a word before dying.

Apu was crying on the speaker phone.

"I want to come home Ani." She wept. "I want to have our baby. Live. I don't want to die. I don't want to die."

I drew circles on my phone. My wife was calling me, crying, afraid, in mortal danger, and I drew circles on my phone.

Goa, 2004

The first time we made love… Goa.

Vagator beach, close to which *Dil Chahta Hai* was filmed, is about 25 km north of Panaji. And further north of it, a third of that distance, is Asvem beach. Apu bulldozed and scared me into staying at Asvem beach when I went to visit her during winter holidays.

I wanted to stay close to her. Near Vagator, where she had her home and also her family eatery, the two built together. But she said "no" and pushed me up north. Apparently, her extended family was spread south from Vagator all the way till Mangalore, with an army of uncles living between Vagator and Panaji. So that part was for me, or rather for us *together*, like the El Prohibido – the forbidden city.

"We are dead if someone sees us," Apu told me darkly.

"Really? How are we gonna die?" Dying for love sounded exciting. *Qayamat se Qayamat tak, Dilli se Goa tak*. Wow!

We were sitting on the bed in a pretty sky blue cottage near the Asvem beach. The cottage had a quaint thatched roof, and I especially liked the two green lanterns hanging on either side of the front door. The blue walls and the thatched roof were giving warmth and shelter to two lovers running away from the eyes of *zaalim zamana*.

"Arrows of the eyes and stones of the words," was Apu's poetic reply.

Yeh lo! And I was thinking the army of uncles would have something more sinister, say at least Rampuri chakus if not AK-47s to terrorise us with. I mocked Apu: "Is it all in eyes and words?"

"Huh?"

"I mean besides the eyes and the words, is there any physical danger? Like your dad chasing me with at least a rifle or something?"

Apu slapped me on the head. "Bhulakkar!" Apparently, she had already told me at least fifty times that her dad Jerry was a total chilled out dude! "Why can't you remember?" she quibbled. "It's the rest of my family that's a problem."

I was incredulous. "But why are they a *problem*? Just because they shoot arrows from eyes and throw stones of words? That's why we are living a hundred miles from each other?"

"I don't know. My cousins *could* attempt an assassination," Apu said.

"Really? Or is that your hypothesis?"

Apu grinned. "Hypothesis."

"Hello! This is not your Maths class! Don't make hypotheses!"

Apu stuck her tongue out. Then she took one of the cream-colored pillows and buried her face in it. She was acting a little different today. More… umm… girlish.

"God! You are such a phattu!" I said. "I never knew that."

"I am not," she said pouting. Dropping down on the bed, she flung her hands and legs apart and lay still.

It was a bewitching sight. Her eyes were closed, her hair was spread over the bed, and she looked… *so open.* Her top had climbed up a little. The swell of her breasts gently went up and down. I swallowed. I had never felt like that before. I mean not that I had never desired her. I had always wanted to kiss her, many many times, and do more. But it's not the same in Aamchi Dilli when you know the only times you are alone, you are on your feet. And if not on your feet, surrounded by a million people.

Now we were alone, in total silence, and she lay on the bed, so… *inviting.* I had an overwhelming desire to bend down and kiss her mad. Those soft lips. The pretty neck. The taut stomach. All of her. I swallowed again and clutched the bedspread. Should I? Should I not? I don't know how much time went by. Seemed like an hour.

I had made up my mind and bent a little when suddenly she opened her eyes and saw me looking at her. Like that. We gazed into each other's eyes without a word for a minute.

I was a phattu as well. I chickened out. "Sleepy?" I asked softly, reaching out to caress a black curl. It was difficult to speak. I felt as if I was full to the neck with something.

"Yes, very." Sighing, she closed her eyes once more and turned the other way, facing away from me. I laid down next to her and stared at the back of her neck.

The next day Apu dragged me to Arambol beach. In Arambol, Apu took me first to the cliff side beach where she told me we would see dolphins leaping in the sea. Fat chance! None of the dolphins were to be seen. Just the gray waves rolling over the gray sea. When the dolphins just refused to show up… lazy bums… Apu suggested we go to the nearby freshwater lake. She said it was a beautiful spot, and it had one thing I would *especially* like.

"Really? What's that?"

"You'll see," she said.

The freshwater lake was a lovely place spotted with banyan trees and a few foreigners trying to be sadhu babas and looking as hideous. Besides that, there were beach shacks; sexy videshi babes showing a lot of their white bodies; and quite a few desi dudes making hay while the gori skin shined, making subhuman noises now and then as they partook of the visual feast.

Instinctively, I put my arm around Apu. Then I looked around me, here and there, but I found nothing that was appealing except for the lake itself.

I turned towards her. "What's there to especially like?"

"Them."

"Who?"

I followed the direction of her finger and found she was pointing at a duo of bikini clad hotties!

I was offended. Who did she think I was? Some despo IITian from her class who would travel two thousand kilometers just to see babes in bikinis? I told her as much. "Kya samajhti hai re tu apun ko?"

She smiled slyly and said wasn't I missing Teena, *my gori*, some time back? (Teena was one of my pretty college juniors who, in one of my rather dumb moments yesterday, I had mentioned to Apu as the fairest girl I had ever seen). Apu thought a couple of more goris memsaabs would help.

Hmm... Time to give it back to her. "But I thought I had made my preferences clear," I replied with a naughty smile as I gazed into her eyes. "I like *saanwli* memsaabs, not gori."

"Saanwli memsaabs?"

'Yes," I said, pretending to ogle Apu head to toe. "And in a bikini."

"Nice try!"

I sighed. "Haal-e-dil hamara... jaane na... bewafa..."

"Ok... ok! I got it!" the saanwli memsaab responded. "Now look there and satisfy yourself with gori memsaabs only."

I sighed again. Dhat teri ki!

Goa, 2004

"Wear it na," I asked my saanwali memsaab.

"Now?"

"Yes... Pleeeeeeeease."

She thought for a second. "Ok... go out of the room."

"Why?" I tried to wriggle out of her marching orders, acting innocent. "See I will turn around and close my eyes." I did that. Then I covered my face with my hands like a good boy. "When you are done changing... just tell me."

But my smartness didn't fly. "High hopes dude! Get out of the room," Apu said, and pushed me out of my blue cottage with the thatched roof.

Crud!

It was Dec 20th, her birthday, and I had given her a Rajasthani lehnga-choli. I had never seen her in that dress, so I told her I presumed she didn't have the desert attire and required one. "You would look good enough to eat after wearing it," I told her impishly. To which Apu made a face. "Ha!" Anyway, all seemed well when I realized we had a problem.

"What problem?" Apu asked.

"You have never worn lehnga-choli before. You won't know how to wear it!"

Memsaab told me to chill. She knew how to wear the dress having borrowed one a few times from a friend in IIT. "Super!" I replied. "Wear it immediately."

"Why?"

I leered. "I want to see you in a sexy dress." Soon after that, despite offering to close my eyes and be the goodest boy ever to ask his girlfriend to change clothes before him, I was pushed out of the room.

"Come in," I heard her say after I pled with her for a long time, after almost twenty minutes had gone by.

"Open the door na!"

"The door is open!"

I pushed the panels and then I realized that… the door was always open; she hadn't latched it. Damn! I could have taken advantage of that! Anyway, as the panels parted, I saw that she was standing in the middle of the room, hands on hips, grinning. *La belle dame sans chunni.*

"How do I look?"

She looked… I took some time to speak out the four letters. I had that full feeling in my throat again. Her shoulders were bare. So was her stomach. The low-cut choli sans the chunni barely contained her… "Sexy…" I managed after a long time.

"So you got your wish." A light smile played on my saanwali memsaab's lips.

We stared at each other. I wanted her… and this time I couldn't stop myself. I closed the door. When I turned back, she hadn't moved. Standing where she was, looking at me in the same way.

Was she waiting for me? I walked upto her and pulled her towards me. She closed her eyes and put her hands on the sides of my neck.

She *was.*

Goa, 2004

Few hours later, we lay snuggled against each other under a blanket. We had made love twice and gone off to a cozy afternoon sleep. She woke up first and woke me up. We made out for a while, then lay quietly just savoring each other's presence. It was an alternate universe in which there is no time unless you call it in. Apu had her back towards me and I lazily grazed the back of her neck with my teeth.

"Ouch! What you doing?"

"I am feeling horny," I told her caressing her arms.

"And your memsaab is feeling hungry," she said pouting.

Shit! She was right. Even I felt hungry. We had skipped lunch - we were so tired after making love.

"What's the time?"

I dug my watch from under the pillow. "Four."

"We have time," she said. Then she took my hand wrapped around her waist and put it over her breast, her hand pressing down on mine. I grinned and kissed her on the back of her shoulder. As I fondled her breast, she said, "Kiss me." I raised myself and turning her face towards me by her chin, I kissed her on her mouth. It was a deep, slow kiss that lasted a long time. "I want you," I whispered when I came up for breath.

"Me too," she whispered back.

Permission granted, I moved down to kiss her whole body.

But as luck would have it, I had a most unromantic interruption. While kissing the hollow of her neck, I got my nose tickled by her golden cross (which she always wore) resting nearby. The inevitable followed – hastily I whirled away from Apu, sat up, and sneezed hard.

Anxious, Apu asked: "What happened?"

"Nothing," I said. "I am ok. It's just your cross."

"What?"

"It's your *cross*. It tickled my nose while I was kissing you."

She stared at me for a second. "Really?"

When I nodded, she responded with a loud giggle. "Makes sense!" she mocked me. "Guess it's protecting me from a bad boy who does bad things to me."

She couldn't stop giggling after that.

"Aisa kya?" I asked, moving down to cover her body with a naughty smile. She nodded with a pinch on my nose.

"Then your cross is not very effective miss," I said cupping her breast. "Because the bad boy," I whispered nibbling her ear, "is going to do the bad things to you anyway."

I had said that too soon. The next second I felt another sneeze coming. I turned around and sneezed a second time, even harder.

Apu giggled again, saying this is what happened to people who questioned her cross' effectiveness. Ya right! "It seems your bad deeds will have to wait sweety," she went on teasing me. "Finish sneezing first."

Look who was talking about bad deeds! This was the same girl who had tried to seduce me *twice* before! I was told the day she had spread herself on my bed, she was actually trying to tempt me into kissing her. She had strategically even worn a tight, low-cut top before coming to my place. But apparently, I acted more shy than a sharmili dulhan: didn't kiss her even when she waved the hint in my face till she was blue! She declared she would have felt insulted if she didn't know how *dumb* I was in these matters.

Sharmili dulhan! Dumb! Talk about feeling insulted!

And I was left with my mouth hanging open when I heard her story - all that was *pre-planned*?!

So I retorted that where bad deeds were concerned, *she* certainly wasn't the one to talk. That was like devil quoting the scriptures! "Who is the seductive temptress?" I asked quirking my brow. Not I.

I thought I was being clever. It didn't occur to me that too clever is often dumb.

"Yes... you are right." Apu sighed, her mood and voice changing in a flash. "At least you don't claim to believe in god." She paused. "Does that make me a hypocrite?"

At first I didn't get it, the change was so sudden. "God? Hypocrite? How do they come here?"

"I seduced you and we are doing it... you know...before... It's supposed to be sin."

I was at once baffled and furious. I had not thought in that direction at all. "No that *doesn't* make you a hypocrite. Why would god..."

She turned her eyes away from me. She wasn't listening. "They say you go to hell for this."

"No… you don't!"

"Will I?"

"Apu… sweety!"

I pulled her face by her chin to bring her gaze back on me. Then I cupped her face in my hands tightly. Bending down, I brought my face within inches of hers.

"What happened?"

"I feel guilty… suddenly."

"Why? We love each other. You love me. Don't you?"

"Yes." She smiled weakly. "Very much." Then she added caressing my hair. "Even more after today."

I smiled back. "Then we should do this every day? Na?" I bent down and kissed her softly.

"Yes." She returned the kiss.

"It can't be wrong right? When it makes you love me more?"

She nodded her head from side to side. "No… good," she said grinning.

I hoped she really believed her words - that she wasn't saying them just to make me feel good. It was not the last time Apu thought she would go to hell.

Mumbai, Nov 27, 2008, 10:02 AM

I had to talk to her. Keep talking to her. Take her mind off Dibbs. I had got to be strong for her. Make sure she didn't lose hope.

"What if I die? Will I go to hell?"

"Apu!"

"Don't shout at me," she said plaintively. "I am trying to be brave and humorous in face of death."

"Ok." I tried to hold my tears back.

"Will I?"

"Why? Did you murder someone?" I asked.

"No."

"Cheated on me?"

"Yes."

"With whom?"

"Cheeni."

"Really?"

"No." She tried to giggle. "Got you, didn't I?"

"No."

"Say yes na," she asked childlike.

"Yes. You got me."

There was silence for moments.

"Then you won't go to hell. You did nothing," I said.

"I did."

"What?"

"I did. *It.*" She tried to giggle again. "Lots of *it.* With you even before marriage. Remember?"

"Yes… And I loved every moment of it!"

"Me too."

"Those were the best days of my life."

There was silence again.

Then she spoke sounding very low. "Will I really go to hell for it?"

"No. You won't!"

I wanted to scream it again. A fierce rage welled inside me. I wanted to break every bone of those who would tell Apu she will go to hell. *Those who murdered Dibbs should go to hell!* I wanted to shout at them - if there is one.

Not Apu. She will not go anywhere. She cannot go anywhere. She cannot die. Please.

Is anyone listening?

Are *you* listening?

Goa, 2004

Two days before Christmas, Apu informed me that we had to visit her dad Jerry in the afternoon. It was my last day in Goa - my flight for Delhi was scheduled next morning. I was refusing to let her go after a great session of love-making, trying to make the most of my last day, when she dropped that bomb.

The news shook me. I was a Bharatiya Nar and having a nice, all-limbs-working-all-bones-intact meeting with girlfriend's progenitor was not exactly in my genes.

So why had Apu set it up?

"Is that the revenge for tearing your buttons?" I asked her. I had tore a couple of her buttons yesterday in spite of trying hard not to. Believe me I had *tried*! We had time, so I ran out and managed to get them fixed.

She kicked me hard.

Ouch! "What?"

"Taking you to meet my dad is not *revenge* dude!"

"Ok! Ok!"

I accepted I was at fault. Apu's dad Mr. Jerry Pinto was sacred territory. Forgetting that was imprudent.

Anyway, I told her I hoped she had at least arranged for me to come out of the meeting alive. If that happened, I swore on my Ducati I would never tear a button of any blouse anymore.

She made a face. "Don't exaggerate dude!" She said before I started feeling too important, I should know that for her dad I was just a friend of hers visiting Goa. She had invited me to lunch as a courtesy; her dad had no clue that I was her guy. So all I had to do was to be a nice boy and eat all that he served me and make sure not to act boyfriendish while he was around… and I would be safe.

Boyfriendish! While Mr. Pinto was around? I would rather behave as if I had been sleeping with my mortal *enemy* for the past three days! "Apu? Kaun Apu?"... Close to that.

Still, there was a problem. Nothing I had brought from Delhi to clothe myself could make me look like a nice boy. All I needed was a heavy gold chain and lo-and-behold! - I could be a perfect replacement for the rapper Eminem. I asked Apu if her dad would be ok sitting with a rapper looking guy on the table instead of a nice boy.

Apu told me to go pour a jug of water on my head. "Chill dude! You look fine!"

"Do I?"

"Yes! And you aren't going for an interview for god's sake!"

Wasn't I? Then why it felt as if I was going for the toughest stress interview of my life?

But there was a ray of hope. The interviewer had no clue about the job I was applying for.

Or at least that's what Apu had told me. Apu! – *the girl with the torn buttons*! What if she was lying? What if this was a plan for the ultimate revenge once-upon-a-time-in-Goa? What if I was grabbed by Mr. Pinto's assistants the moment I entered her house and stripped and skinned and sliced and diced and baked and caked and tossed and sauced and served on the table with forks and knives? What if?

When I asked her that, Apu refused to provide me an answer and instead, threatened to leave my place. She said my headless-*creative*-chicken act was getting on her nerves. A headless chicken was bad in itself. But a headless chicken trying to be creative? – that was unbearable!

I quickly apologized to Apu. Whatever the future may bring, I desperately needed support and insider information from the enemy camp.

Jerry Pinto turned out to be an interesting man at first sight, somewhat of a character you saw in movies. He had curly graying hair cropped short and a well-trimmed graying beard, wide forehead with four distinct creases, deep sunken eyes, sharp nose and thin lips. He was about a couple of inches shorter than me and much stouter. Wearing a rimless spectacle, he would have looked a merciless university professor – one of those kinds who take sadistic pleasure in giving you a 'D' – than a restaurateur if it had not been for his high collared jacket and a thick metallic silver chain hanging from his neck (and *I* was worrying about looking like a rapper!).

Well… for now he looked more like a Hollywood fisherman about to start on an expedition in the cold, stormy high seas. I hoped I was not the bait he planned to take along with him to feed to the fishes.

"Hello, I am Jerry Pinto," he greeted me with a wide smile and shook my hand energetically when we met in his restaurant – which was mostly empty as it was afternoon. That didn't exactly increase my confidence level.

But thank god – he look much less merciless when he smiled!

"Hi, I am Aniruddh." I smiled back deferentially, trying to sound as nice a boy as possible.

"You are Aparajita's classmate?"

So Apu had told him next to nothing. I didn't know whether to be pleased or displeased.

"No… I study in a different college. St. Stephen's."

From his face, it seemed he hadn't heard of my famed institution. So I explained further: "It's a college in Delhi University. I study Economics there."

"Papa knows St. Stephens," Apu interjected. "He himself was a student of JNU."

Crud! Was that true? I didn't know I was *that* bad at face reading!

Hastily, I tried to make up. "What did you study there Uncle?" Or should have I called him papa-in-law?

"Nothing," he grinned. He explained he had gone there to do an M.A. in English, but actually ended up studying next to nothing. "I was tired of Goa and just wanted to get out. Roam around India a bit." JNU was his excuse and Delhi was his base-camp from where he covered the entire north and north-east - from Ladakh to Arunachal.

"Had lots of fun. I passed though. Barely." He grinned wider.

Ok. Could someone explain to me how had Apu got through IIT with *such* inspiration?

But umm… I had to finally agree with her. Jerry Pinto did look like a chilled out dude – very unlikely to chase me around Goa with a rifle in hand. I relaxed.

For some reason, Mr. Pinto had already decided I was a Punjabi. I have no clue what gave him that impression, but the result of that misunderstanding was a huge Punjabi lunch that Mr. Pinto said he had got specially prepared for me because I must be missing Punjabi food in Punjabi-forsaken Goa. "Here is makki di roti, here is sarson da saag," he proudly announced placing before me a couple of humongous rotis and a bowl full of saag. The rest of the dishes would soon follow.

What! How? And I was expecting a lavish Goan fare considering I was sitting in the restaurant of a well-known Goan chef. I gnashed my teeth at Apu while Mr. Pinto was busy buttering my rotis. She got the point and shrugged. "Not me! I never told him anything like that."

"What?" Mr. Pinto looked up at both of us - one from the other – confused.

"Nothing!" I said hastily, shaking my head with a high frequency. It was paramount for me to be in good graces of Mr. Pinto, and a sure shot way to ruin my chances was to make a sumptuous dinner (even if Punjabi) made by a proud chef like him feel unwelcome.

But he had caught it. "You aren't a Punjabi?" he asked me.

I preferred to be wordless. Or perhaps the time was not enough for my brain to send adequate signal to my mouth. It was Apu who replied. "No, he isn't a Punjabi! When did I say he was a Punjabi?"

Jerry Pinto's face fell. Crud! "Oh! I thought he was a Punjabi.. thought Hiranis were Punjabis," he said in a sorry voice and with a sorrier face. He turned to me. "So you don't like-."

"No!" I interrupted him forcefully. Of course I liked Punjabi food. I was a Sindhi, but weren't Punjab and Sindh right next to each other? - Brothers. Similar were their cuisines - sisters. Absolutely. Liking one was liking the other. No difference.

Thank god, Mr. Pinto had little knowledge of Sindhi cuisines and took me at my word! For that matter, I didn't tell him I didn't like Sindhi cuisine much either.

The coup-de-grace was yet to come. Through the lunch we chitchatted about my Goa trip for which I had to think carefully before giving any answer - so I could omit Apu from every detail. What galled me was that the girl for whom I was taking such pains was grinning wide at my lies from across the table – having a ball at my expense the entire time. If that wasn't enough, she kept inserting such annoying comments such as "*Really?*" (as if she didn't already know all I was saying!), "*That's strange! Nobody goes that far to stay,*" (even more annoying given she was the one who forced me to stay that far!), and "*Tch… I could have taken you to better places,*" (after having dragged me to the supposedly 'worse' places by singing paeans to them!). At last, the serial offender got up to give finishing touches to the desserts and I was left alone with Mr. Jerry Pinto.

That's when I got a jor ka jhatka that jor se laga! I was happily finishing the last few morsels of a mix of pulao and chicken tikka masala (yes, the lunch was stereotypical Punjabi though the dishes were prepared really well) when Mr. Pinto turned to me and said: "You are Apu's boyfriend, aren't you?" He had a soft smile on his lips.

I forgot chewing. My mouth full, I stared at him like a deer caught in the headlights. Guess it was time for getting *Khallas…ed*! The assistants would now emerge from the kitchen, and strip and skin and slice and dice and bake and cake and toss and sauce and serve me on the table with pulao and chicken tikka masala!

I swallowed and looked around hoping to see a few more customers. There were none! Except for yours truly! The few who were there when I came in had left! "Umm… Uncle… I…" I fumbled through the words.

He cut in after the three disjointed words, telling me not to worry. "Say the truth. I won't be angry."

I won't be angry! Was that believable? He was a Bharatiya Nar too, and having a nice, all-limbs-working-all-bones-intact meeting with the female offspring's boyfriend was not in *his* genes either.

But what choice I had with Mr. Dad sitting in the front? It was too late to deny the charge without appearing to commit the crime of lying also.

"Yes sir," I nodded. The "sir" part came out of my mouth automatically.

"Don't call me sir," he grinned. "Call me Jerry now."

I nodded wordlessly. *Call him Jerry*! Who did he think I was... recipient of Mahaveer Chakra?

"Are you wondering how I knew?"

Not at all Jerry! I am wondering about slightly different things - say the assistants in the kitchen. How many do you have? How tall are they, how well-built? Do they go to the gym? Do they fear the police and law? How strongly do they believe in Christ's message of love, non-violence and universal brotherhood? *Those* are the questions that are currently occupying my mind!

"I don't remember Apu calling any guy for lunch for a long time. So I knew you must be a *special* friend," he went on.

Oh! So it was all because Miss Aparajita Pinto was stupid enough to do something *this* telltale! What was she thinking? Or maybe knowing Apu, she had done this on purpose - let her papa get the hint without having to announce it officially. Except that she had not counted on papa interrogating me, and me spilling the beans and making it official.

Ha ha! I was pleased. It was a perfect revenge for Apu making me the bakra. Now let her get a not so nice surprise when she came back from the kitchen. Ha!

But before Apu came back from the kitchen, it was I who got a surprise from Mr. Pinto.

"My daughter has been very happy for some time, especially in the last few days," he suddenly said. "I have not seen her *this* happy since her mother died."

I jerked out of my thoughts, and cursed myself for not paying attention. This was serious. He sounded a little pensive. I kept silent, not knowing what to say.

He went on. "It hit Apu hard… her mother's death. She told you how it happened?"

I nodded.

For some reason he was pleased. "Good." He paused. "Tell me Aniruddh… since when did you guys come together… I mean… you know, when did you become her boyfriend. Was it sometime towards the end of last year?"

I was taken aback. How did he know?

"Yes. That's when we started dating," I said.

"Seemed like that. Apu's voice started sounding happier since then."

I stayed mum. I was beginning to feel strange inside – as if my heart had started filling up again. It was not exactly happiness. More like I wanted to grip Mr. Pinto's hands in mine for some time. Then go to Apu and give her a very tight hug.

"Thank you sir."

"No… I should thank *you*," he replied. "You have made her happy. And don't call me "sir". Call me Jerry."

"Thank you Jerry."

He smiled. "Will you do me a favor?"

I sat straight. "Anything sir… Jerry."

"I don't like Delhi. Rather what it's become nowadays. Keep Apu safe and happy for me, will you?"

I smiled. "I will Jerry."

"Your parents wouldn't mind?"

That was out of the blue. My heart stopped beating for a couple of seconds. I looked deeply into his eyes. Was he testing me? His eyes were fathomless.

"In the beginning... yes."

"But you would uh... bring them around?"

"I *definitely* will."

He smiled wider. "I like you. You know why?"

I said a "no" with my head.

"Because when they really matter - you are a man of few words."

I smiled at the compliment. It was I guess a big one. "Thank you Jerry."

Soon we saw Apu walking out of the kitchen door with the dessert in hand. "She is coming. Safe and happy... remember. Promise?"

I nodded.

Mumbai, Nov 27, 2008, 11:45 AM

He was the first to come. We shook hands. Then he stood next to me without a word.

I looked at my watch. "She'll message in about ten minutes," I said.

He nodded.

We were silent for a while.

"I know my Apu. She's my girl. Strong. She'll defeat the terrorists. She'll make it."

I looked at him. He sat bent forward, looking down at the ground, hands clutched tightly. He suddenly looked old. I reached out and gripped his arm. "I am sorry."

He turned his head. "Why?"

Why? Bitterness rose up my throat. *Safe and happy?* If only he knew.

He squeezed my hand back. "You couldn't have done anything."

I could have Jerry. Yes, I could have. She wouldn't be here if I would have. She would be safe and happy.

"She'll make it, won't she?" This time it was a plaintive question.

I closed my stinging eyes. I don't know Jerry, I don't know.

Delhi, 2005

Soon after we came back from Goa, I switched from my bikes to driving around a Honda CR-V. Mostly. I mean I still loved my pretty machines, but kissing Apu while leaning against them was difficult. I mean not physically. Socially - without raising eyebrows. We were in bloody conservative Delhi!

I never got to spend much time with Apu, so we wanted to make the most of what we had together. Making out, without anyone noticing it, was far easier in a SUV than on a bike. Ultimately, between my bikes and Apu's kisses, I chose Apu's kisses, the biking brotherhood be damned.

But the frequency of those kisses had declined worryingly. As her second quiz approached, the time my girl was willing to give me went down. A lot. At least that's what it felt. Apu said she would come out with me only on Sundays! Her grades had gone down last semester and she had to study hard to pull them up.

I rebelled and argued in vain. I mean why in the world people have to study so much. Wasn't she an eight pointer anyway? After spending so much time with a woman of their tribe, I had become familiar with IITD ways. And I knew that for the specialization Apu was in, a GPA of 8.3 was pretty good.

But my pulse didn't melt before Apu… dal nahin gali. "I am not a genius like you," she retorted and told me to take a hike. Not even when I threatened her that I will fill her throat with hickeys next time we kissed. "Be my guest," she said – Dibbs, a senior, had taught her how to hide hickeys with a concealer, so it didn't matter. Damn Dibbs!

By the time Apu's quizzes finished, I was so desperate for my girl that I even thought about filing a case in the Supreme Court for *restitution of boyfriend's rights.* I mean I had heard they had a law like that for husbands… shouldn't there would be one for boyfriends too? If not that, at least a PIL against exams being held thrice a semester which was a clear violation of human rights.

We young lovers are also humans, aren't we? Even though most of country may behave as if that wasn't true. Where is Ms. Roy when you *really* need her?

Well… I didn't have to file a PIL. Apu promised me the day her last quiz of *Digital Signal Processing* finished, (Man did they have scary subject names!) we would go out every evening, and she would spend the entire weekend with me in Rohan's farmhouse. Yippee!

Since we had come back from Goa, there were times when we couldn't have enough of each other. Rohan's Mehrauli farmhouse was where we took refuge from the zaalim eyes of zamana when we were in that mood.

The Friday her exams finished and we went to the farmhouse, I brought my Triumph along. Apu had told me to – she said she wanted to ride my bike. We would be with each other at the end of the evening anyway, so kisses were not an issue, and I agreed to her demand. While returning from PVR where we had gone to watch a movie, it began to rain. I thought we could take temporary refuge in a coffee shop and I was about to stop when Apu declared she wanted to ride in the rain. "You have pakaofied me a hundred times by talking about riding in the rain," she said, "let me do it too."

"This is not *rain*!" I said. This was just a shower.

"Whatever. I want to get wet."

I chuckled. She had given me a nice opening to pull her leg.

"Get wet right now? Can't wait till we reach the farmhouse?" I asked laughing.

Getting what I meant, Apu pulled my ear hard from behind.

"Ouch!"

"Yes… right now baby," she said. Then when we got to the farmhouse, she would be in a hurry to take her clothes off. Did I want that?

Hmm… I wanted that. *Of course* I wanted that. I raced my bike in the rain, eager to reach the farmhouse, while Apu got wet behind me, singing full throatedly… *rimjhim gire sawan…* as we went past her campus.

By the time we reached the farmhouse, we were totally drenched and shivering. Not a problem. The chowkidar Balli Bhaiya, who knew us well, was expecting us; Rohan had told him we were coming. As we walked through the hall to our room, Apu suddenly grabbed my hand and pulled me close.

"What?"

"You said I would be in *trouble* as soon as we were alone," she said quite seriously. "Didn't you?"

Hmm…! The thing was that she had made me pine for her for about a month now, so I had threatened her with passionate revenge as soon as I got her alone.

Then her face changed. In a flash. She said with a sultry smile. "We *are* alone."

I grinned. "Impatient… are we?"

"Yessss," she said biting her lower lip. "I am wet… and in a hurry to take my clothes off."

We had not had a single kiss in a fortnight. So the result of our aloneness was a liplock that continued (broken only when I was kissing her neck or she was biting my ears) until we reached our room. I managed to open the latch with one hand while holding Apu's hair by the other. Then we dragged ourselves in, still kissing.

I groped for the light switch with one hand.

Apu broke the kiss. "Don't turn on the light."

"Why?"

"I already asked Balli Bhaiya for a candle. Must be there on the table."

When I turned around after lighting the candle, Apu stood smiling, her left knee over the bed. She had taken her t-shirt off. With a wicked grin, she flicked off a drop of water that was running down her stomach. "See… I am sooooo… wet."

We didn't even dry ourselves before plunging into a candlelight romance. And more. Much more.

Delhi, 2005

That hadn't been a wise decision – not drying ourselves. When I woke up next morning, rather late, I had a splitting headache. I could feel my ears on fire. Apu was opening the windows and drawing back the curtains to let the sunlight in. "Get up lazy bum," she chirped. "It's already ten." We had planned to go on a drive to Surajkund.

"Don't do that," I whined hoarsely drawing the quilt over my head tight. "I don't feel good."

Apu came running and put her hand on my forehead. "Bloody hell!" she cried. "You are running temperature! High. At least 102!"

"Tell me." My head was burning like the fires of Spanish Inquisition!

Immediately, Apu went off to find Balli Bhaiya to ask him to fetch a thermometer. But as I had predicted, she came back fretting - there was no thermometer in the farmhouse. Then she asked me for my bike keys.

Even with 102^0 temperature, I sat up. "What?"

Apu thought I hadn't understood her. So she explained that she needed my bike to go buy a thermometer, few Crocin tablets, and anything else the pharmacist suggested. And that I better not be a hero and lay down quietly.

"I am not asking *that.* Have you ever ridden a bike?" I whispered. That too, my bike was a Triumph.

"I have ridden scooters."

I didn't know whether to laugh or cry. Perhaps crying would have been better given my eyes were already tearful. "Tell me you are joking! They are not even close!"

"I know," said my sweetheart anxiously. "But I will try."

"Try?" Had she gone nuts? "Try how?"

"Don't worry. I have brief experience on bikes too."

Her brief experience, it turned out, was *trying out her cousin's Yamaha for a few days*. That too not alone, but with his active assistance from behind! "I hope I remember something." She shrugged. "We have no choice anyway- Balli Bhaiya says there is nothing in walking distance."

I almost grinned - imagining Apu trying out my Triumph with her 'brief experience'. I may have even let her if it wasn't so risky.

Man! She was quite the action hero! My headache half forgotten, I told her to come nearer. "Stupid! Why do *you* have to go?' I pulled her down on the bed with a sudden tug when she came near.

"Ouch! What you doing?"

"Mujhe chhor ke mat jao meri jaan!" I said attempting to get my arm around her. I didn't want to say to her directly that her brief experience was not quite enough to ride my Triumph. It could have proved counter-effective with my headstrong girl.

She straight-armed me. "Hands off dude! Try romancing me after you get well!"

God! She could be totally like Hitler at times! "Ok! But stay with me."

"Hello! Who will get the thermometer? Crocin?"

Thermometer and Crocin? - How I itched to tell her poetically that they would be useless without our *pyar*. And our pyar would be in deep peril if she attempted to ride my Triumph on Delhi roads!

"Tell Balli Bhaiya no. I want you here. For my sewa!"

"How will Bhaiya go? On his bicycle?"

"No, on my bike!" I exclaimed at last. "I have seen *him* riding. Which I sure can't say for you!"

Apu gave me an injured, dekh-loongi-tujhe type look, but to my relief, she finally handed over the baton of shopping to Balli Bhaiya. Thank god!

Apu had declared she would feed me broth the whole day to help me in my fight with fever. I guess that was the punishment for not letting her ride my bike. Girls always do this - devise a clever home-made punishment if they can't get their way with you. So after Balli Bhaiya arrived, in spite of my protests, my girl retired to the kitchen to make the broth while I stewed in silence.

This went on the whole day: broth making. Balli Bhaiya made full use of my Triumph and made two more trips to the market to buy vegetables and chicken and what not. I guess he was enjoying the whole show. "*Didi aapka bada khayal rakhti hain*," – he informed me twice.

Not *me* so much! I was fed - and yes, I counted in spite of my fever and occasional snoozing – five different types of broths: chicken, mutton and pure veg. Even though all of them were tasty, I told Lady Dhanwantri that my fever would leave me faster if she sat by me and fed me more of her love and affection instead of feeding me her experimental broth recipes!

"Shut up!" Lady Dhanwantri answered. "I would give you enough love and affection if you chupchap eat all I give you and get well soon."

"Like last night?" I asked.

She grinned - last night had been memorable in more than one way. "Yup, like last night," she said affectionately.

Ooh la la... Now how could I not try to be absolutely 'chupchap'?

But the fever stayed in spite of the broth diet. Next morning, it was 101... still. What I didn't tell Apu - who was worrying over me and which I was enjoying a lot - that my headache and throat ache were almost gone, perhaps courtesy the broths.

"See I told you..." I pouted to her like a kid. "... the broths wouldn't help. You should have fed me romance!"

Ignoring me and my theatrics, a worried Apu watched over me sitting right by my bed till it was almost noon. But the fever didn't come down. "I think we should go to a doctor," – she finally decided, ready to abdicate her medical throne. And then, while Apu was fretting and insisting on going to the doctor and I was playing the childlike invalid and enjoying all the attention I was getting from her, Rohan's mom arrived unexpectedly.

Delhi, 2005

Suddenly we heard a female voice say something at full volume to Balli Bhaiya in the corridor. I didn't even have enough time to curse Rohan for not informing us before Sheetal auntie was at our door. She saw us and froze. Under her wide-eyed gaze, I was soon wishing for Harry Potter's cloak of invisibility.

Apu's situation was worse. I, at least, was under a blanket. In contrast, Apu was out there not even dressed completely. Then she was a girl.

And auntie didn't know her.

Four... five deafeningly silent seconds went by. It was Apu who found her voice first.

"Hi auntie."

Auntie ignored Apu and turned to me.

"Hi," she said back. That was a rather frosty hi. Didn't sound as if Auntie was full of joy at meeting us. "Rohan didn't tell me you were here."

"He didn't?" I feigned innocence.

"No."

"Oh!"

I had little choice, so I lied to auntie that we had come here yesterday evening to have a small party. "Then I caught fever because I got drenched in the rain. We had to stay on." At least that part was true.

'You have fever?"

I nodded, my face looking miserable, as wretched I could make it to awaken auntie's motherly feelings in her large bosom. Now I am a good actor, and I had somewhat succeeded in my goal when the charm was unluckily broken by Apu. "Yes auntie… it's as high as 102!" she piped up from the side, perhaps thinking she should say something to help me.

Crud! Auntie shifted her gaze on Apu with a *and-who-the-hell-are-you* kind of expression.

"My friend… Apu," I hastily introduced Apu to the *not so sheetal* looking Sheetal auntie.

"Friend? Really?" Sheetal auntie's icy tone said volumes. I saw she was sampling Apu from top to down.

I was baffled. I mean I could understand auntie getting surprised by our presence. Maybe even upset – she was a slightly conservative character. But *this* didn't make sense. She was not just upset… she was furious! Boiling like lava. Why?

Then in a flash I got it. Shit! Auntie perhaps thought I had hired Apu - she was a… I almost said the 'f' word aloud. "Apu studies in IIT Delhi… auntie," I rushed the fact out. "She stayed back to care for me because of the fever."

When she heard the IIT word, I saw Sheetal auntie's face visibly relax; and the creases around her eyes smoothened. Thank god! Yet she prodded Apu further: "What do you study there… beta?"

"Electrical Engineering," said Apu. I hoped she too had got the hang of the queer situation we were in.

Auntie was almost smiling now. "Nice beta… and thanks for taking care of Aniruddh," she told Apu. "He is almost like my own son." She smiled wider at me and I sighed with relief.

It was not long after that we left the place. Auntie insisted that she would drop both of us at our respective residences in her car. My Triumph would follow me the next day after spending a day in the care of Balli Bhaiya.

After we reached Kailash hostel, I realized Auntie still wasn't easy about Apu. "Can I see your room?" she asked Apu. Apu was surprised, but agreed with pleasure. I don't know what happened inside, but Auntie came out beaming. "Very good girl," Auntie nodded happily to me as took her seat beside me in the car. "Very intelligent," she went on.

Was she endorsing our relationship or what?

That turned out to be wishful thinking. "But she is a Christian... no?" auntie added soon as we were crossing the IIT main gate.

I guess that sort of tagging is mandatory in our goddamned country. @#%$#@#!

And then it struck me - auntie wasn't just asking me a rhetorical question. She was also making a statement by way of that. That Apu was indeed a good and intelligent girl, and great girlfriend material, and all that was fine... But she was a Christian, so how had I actually made her my girlfriend?

I shouldn't have said anything in return, let the matter rest, but my caustic nature got the better of me.

"That's ok Auntie," I sassed her. "I am also not a Hindu."

She looked shocked. "You already converted?"

I almost laughed at the horrified expression on her face. "No... but I am an atheist auntie. *Nastik*."

Throughout the drive, there was a frown on auntie's face. She didn't talk to me after that, except for a soft "bye" when I got out at my home. I reciprocated in kind.

And then, as I walked into my room, the scary part dawned on me. I had acted like a damn fool! In trying to needle Sheetal auntie, I may have led her to think it was because of Apu I had turned my back upon my own gods. She may not have understood that the atheism thing was a philosophical stance, that it had nothing to do with Apu. Shit!

Auntie knew maa well. What if she…?

Delhi, 2005

"But why are you so afraid of maa knowing?"

"I just don't want her to know… or dad."

"But why? I mean even Kruti di… Vishu Bhaiya… all of them had love marriages. Maa may not be happy if she isn't a Sindhi, but she won't kill you right?"

"It's not so simple."

"Why!"

"She is a Catholic!"

Aaru's mouth opened and she clapped her fingers over it. "Oh…. Oh."

She was silent for a few moments. Then: "Bro?"

"Yes."

"You are in trouble."

I sighed. "I know."

Delhi, 2005

In many fairy tales, there is an evil witch that tries to tempt the girl away from the guy with an exotic looking red fruit and is stopped at the last moment. Happened with us too. In our case, the evil witch was a university called UCLA – the University of California, Los Angeles. One of the famous universities of the world. And she tempted Apu with a PhD in electrical engineering.

I know I am talking nonsense; I guess I was just too furious to think straight when I came to know about it.

I had to blame someone… something. Not Apu.

I don't think even now I can blame her for thinking of leaving me for five whole years. She didn't know where I wanted our relationship to go. Even I didn't. Like an ostrich I was avoiding the inevitable. Hoping things would sort out by themselves. Like magic. Of course they wouldn't have.

I guess Apu had sensed it. That I still feared my parents – what they would say when they found out about us. Sometimes I had even talked to her about my fears – what would happen, say, if Sheetal auntie revealed our story to mom. *But isn't she a Christian*? And all that.

That had left her unsure perhaps - we had never discussed the future explicitly. And though she had told me many times she didn't want to go for higher studies (electrical engineering bored her she said), in those stressful times, UCLA perhaps gave her a way out. A sort of support. What if?

The secret came out in Gill Uncle's drawing room one Saturday when on his request, Apu had made Bhindi Masala. Actually, it was not a request. Apu had let out that she could make awesome Bhindi Masala, so we had bulldozed her into cooking it for us.

Midway through the yummy meal, I decided to rob Apu of some of her Bhindi with a surprise attack. It was revenge for her accusing me earlier of trying to steal her recipe.

"No!" Apu yelled as soon as I grabbed a few pieces from her bowl. "Give it back!"

"Someone was accusing me of trying to steal their recipe..." I reminded her slyly.

"You *were* stealing!"

"Ok. Then I will also steal the result of that recipe. The *delicious* result of that recipe," I needled her, dropping a big stolen piece in my mouth. "Ahh... yumm...my."

"Chor!"

"Yup," I replied smugly. "Once a chor, always a chor."

Apu had no answer to that. She changed track and became the distressed damsel. "Please... please... Ani. I am hungry."

I didn't melt. "Take some more roti," I suggested to her. And if she was still hungry, there was kheer too. But no, I wasn't going to part with my stolen booty.

Apu looked annoyed. "I may not get to eat Bhindi Masala for the next five years! *Gimme my Bhindi*!" she cried.

"Why? You don't get Bhindi Masala in IIT mess?"

"No... but you obviously don't get Bhindi Masala in the US of A," she retorted.

"US of A?"

What the hell she was talking about? And from the way she clamped her lips immediately, I sensed this was not something she had intended to mention.

"You are going to USA? For *five years*?" I asked.

... ...

"Why are you going to *USA*?"

"I don't know if I am going yet."

"What does that *mean*?"

Apu looked away from Gill Uncle and me. Seconds went by.

"Apu?"

"I have applied for PhD," ..." she confessed slowly, still looking away. " I may get through… I don't know."

"But you said… And…What's this Apu?" I saw Gill Uncle signaling me to calm down. I ignored him. "Why you didn't even tell me?"

Gill Uncle got up. "I will leave you two."

Apu turned to him. "It's ok… We…"

"No, I will go," Gill Uncle said. "And don't forget to finish your dinner you guys." He walked out on to the porch.

I turned back towards Apu. She was looking down. "When did this happen?"

"Nothing has *happened*."

"When did you apply?"

… … … … … … …

"Apu?"

"Last month!"

"Why?"

… … … … … … …

"Didn't you say you would take a job here after you finished?"

… … … … … … …

"Apu?"

"I am sorry! I don't know!"

She was still looking down.

"What don't you KNOW?"

I was raising my voice. It happened on its own.

"I don't know," she replied. "I don't know where we will be after this year. You will fly off to someplace like London School of Economics. I also want to do something. Not stay back and just pine for you!"

"Is that it?"

Apu hesitated for a couple of moments. Then she said yes.

"I don't think so," I said. "But if that is all… if it has nothing to do with the fact that I am a Hindu and you a Christian… and nothing to do with the fact that you think I am rich and you are poor… and nothing to do with the fact that you still don't believe that I will never let those things come between us… then you have nothing to be worried about. I am *not* going to LSE."

I sounded angry. Which was good. I wanted to.

Apu looked at me at last. With sad eyes.

"Ani, I don't want it to happen like that. I…"

"I do."

"But it's your dream Ani…"

"Dreams change! I got my dream. I got *you.*"

She looked away.

"Apu! Say something! Don't you believe me?"

… … … … … … …

"Apu!" I was getting panicky.

She turned her face. Small teardrops glistened in her eyes.

I clutched her hands tight and pulled her towards me. I gazed into her eyes. "I changed my mind about LSE Apu… ok? I will do anything for you. Just don't leave me… ok?"

She nodded. "I am sorry. I was just scared that…."

"I know," I stopped her. "It's my fault. I should have told you before. Sorry I didn't. But I am telling it now. I don't want LSE. *I don't want*

LSE. I want you."

I smiled to make her happier. I wanted to see her smile.

"No, it wasn't your faul…"

"Shoo!" I stopped her again. Then I lifted my hands to wipe away her tears. "All that matters is I am not going anywhere. I am happy with you. F**k economics!"

She flinched, surprised for a moment.

"Yes. *F**k* economics," I repeated.

She smiled through her tears. "What about your plans to tour India on your bike? Che Guevera style?"

I smiled back. "That? That is still there. Only one change - I am thinking of taking you along. Behind me. *She* Guevera. We will start the revolution together."

"What?"

"Don't want that?" I asked her. "I figured." I put my fingers on her lips. "Then don't ever… ever… ever ever talk about going away. Anywhere. Ok?"

There was a small silence. "Ok."

"Promise?"

"Yes." She kissed my fingers still resting on her lips. I withdrew them, bent down and tried to give her a soft kiss.

"No!" She stopped me and pushed me back.

"Why?"

"Gill Uncle may be watching *and* you have Bhindi on your lips."

That reminded me of something. I looked down at my bowl. "So no need to return your Bhindi… right?"

I looked up to find Apu grinning. "Greedy pig!" she exclaimed. "Gimme my Bhindi!" She tried to snatch the bowl from me.

"Noooo…!"

Things were finally all right. I had defeated the evil witch.

Mumbai, Nov 27, 2008, 5:55 AM

Rohan gave his phone to me. "Your dad," he said.

I took it. "Hello!"

"Sonu bête?"

He sounded anxious. Aarushi must have…

"Yes dad?"

"Are you ok beta?"

Ok? Apu was perhaps dying… But why would he care?

"Sonu?"

"Yes dad, I am ok."

"And Aparajita?"

I almost laughed. What wouldn't I give to know?

"I don't know dad. Apu is hurt, a little, but she is alive. I know that much."

"Bête. I am so sorry. I am coming there. We are catching the next flight."

"Thanks dad."

What else?

He went on. "Everything will be fine bete. Apu will be fine. I have never even seen her. God will not let this happen." His voice caught. "I will see bahu. I know I will see bahu. You must not lose hope. You must pray. Pray to Hanuman. He is Sankatmochan. He rescued Sita from the Asuras." Dad was rushing like the Rajdhani express. It was very unlike him - the composed and methodical guy. Composed, even at the moment I had walked out on him. "You must pray to him. He would help bahu also. He…"

"Dad!"

"No, listen to me. Pray. *For once*. It will help. To Sankatmochan…"

He suddenly paused.

"And pray to… Jesus also. And Mary. To everyone. All gods are same. There is no difference. I am praying to everyone to save bahu."

In spite of everything, I almost smiled.

"I know I will see her, give her my aashirwaad. I know they will all listen to me. I know." There was a moment's silence. Then his voice shook. "I am sorry Sonu. I should have come earlier."

Delhi, 2005

There were two problems in telling my parents about Apu.

One, I couldn't tell them I would run away and marry her. Indian Law wouldn't have allowed me. I wasn't 21 yet.

Two, I had to tell them anyway, and I had no clue how to do it.

I thought of breaking the news over the dinner table, but then dropped the idea. Seemed too abrupt. Then I thought of asking Aaru to be my messenger, but stopped again - it felt cowardly. I also thought of scheduling a session with my parents. But even that seemed too dramatic. Finally, I decided to tell my parents separately. To maa first, then dad.

I came straight to the point the afternoon I talked to maa. She was wordless for sometime after I told her that I loved a Christian girl and would like to marry her soon after I graduated next year. (I would be 21 then).

"Your dad knows?" she asked at last.

"No."

"Talk to him then. I know you won't listen to me."

"What if I don't listen even to him maa?" I asked.

Maa didn't give me any answer. After she left the room, I realized she had asked nothing more about Apu. Knowing that she was a Christian I guess was enough.

A few days before I talked to dad I thought of consulting Rohan. I mean I was fairly sure of the outcome, but I didn't know what I would do after that. I mean I knew dad would likely say "no", but then?

Rohan kept quiet after he heard me, apparently thinking over the problem while he bounced a basketball.

"Tell me *something* dude!" I exclaimed after a while.

Rohan looked at me. "You sure you wanna do this?"

"Do I have a choice?"

"Why can't you wait for a while? Graduate. Take up a job. Then tell. I mean what's the hurry?"

I smiled mirthlessly. "Why? So when I have to walk out anyway, I don't have to scrounge for roti, kapda, makan because I have a job?"

Rohan threw the basketball at my face. "You won't have to scrounge for anything as long as I am there!"

I caught the basketball just in time before it hit me. "Thanks dude. For the support. But why are you trying to ruin my thobra?"

He grinned. "If I ruin your thobra, Apu will leave you." He said then I won't have to tell my dad anything. "Problem solved. Na rahega bamboo, na bajegi flute."

Bastard! Trying to be humorous even when I was in such deep shit. "Thanks! I never knew you had such long-term vision!" I told him curling my lip.

"Most welcome buddy. Always thinking the best for you."

Talking to Rohan had cleared up at least one thing for me – if things didn't work out, I wasn't going to stay with my parents just so I could leave them when I got a job. If Apu was not welcome in my home, I had to leave it immediately.

Well… that's what I did.

Delhi, 2005

The day I went to tell him about Apu, my dad was working late in his home office. He was bent over his work when I entered his room. I asked him if I could talk to him. It was something important.

"Wait for half an hour," he said without looking up.

"Dad, it's really important."

He replied, still looking down, that he knew what I had come to talk about. Maa had told him. "Wait for some time," he insisted. "I am also working on something important."

I shrugged and went back to my room. Almost an hour later, Aaru poked her head through the door and said dad was calling me downstairs to his office. So I went to him again.

"What is the girl's name?" he asked without any preamble the moment I sat in the visitor's chair.

"Aparajita."

"I thought she was a Christian," he said. "That's what your maa told me."

"Yes, she is."

"How old are you?"

"What?" The abruptness of the question took me by surprise.

"I am asking your age Sonu." (Sonu was my pet name).

Didn't he know that very well? Then why the natak? "I will be twenty-one next February."

"Which means you are twenty now."

I stayed silent. I wasn't about to answer his rhetorical questions just to humor him.

"Have you been married before?"

I stared at him. What on earth was that supposed to mean?

"I think not," he went on after a brief pause. "And at twenty, young people have no idea what marriage means or what one should want from marriage. Neither do you. That's why you have come to me with such a foolish thought."

That was more or less the gist of all that came afterwards: that I was a hot-blooded fool to fall in love with Apu and think of marrying her; that intelligent men (like him?) let the elders decide who they should marry because the elders had experience with institutions like marriage; that if he let me go ahead with my stupid decision, I was going to regret it soon.

"When I was your age," he told me, "I wasn't thinking about marriage. I was thinking of how to take my father's business forward."

"But you got married when you were twenty-two."

"Yes, but I let my parents think about that."

He concluded that's exactly what he wanted from me. Focus on finishing college, and then focus on our family business. They (meaning I guess he and maa) would get me married to the right girl when the right time came.

Yeah… right. I should have expected that. Didn't they always want everything proper and *right*?

"Dad… you haven't asked me a thing about Apu."

"Who?"

"Apu... Aparajita."

"Do I need to?"

I braced myself to say it. "Yes, you do. She is going to be your daughter-in-law."

He sat up. "Sonu... didn't you hear me? I want you to forget this foolish idea."

"Dad-"

He cut me off. "Didn't you plan to go LSE? That's what you told me a year back."

So now he was going to play the LSE card. A year ago, I clearly remembered how irritated he had got when I told him I wanted to go to LSE.

"I dropped the idea."

"You dropped the idea? Why?"

What was he aiming at? I was getting tired of the questions.

"I want to stay here."

"Stay here? And do what?"

I shrugged. "Help you... or take up a job."

"Who made you change your plan? The girl?"

I stayed silent. It was useless telling him that actually it was the other way round.

"I knew it," he said leaning back in his chair. "She's got you trapped."

"Dad! Please don't talk about Apu like that!"

"I am just stating the truth," he said calmly. "You are just doing what she wants."

"I have to go dad." I started to get up.

"Wait. I am not done," he commanded.

I stood looking down at him.

"Sit down. I will not let you spoil your life like this."

I kept standing.

"You will not marry that girl. You will go for higher studies and forget her."

No, dad. That's not going to happen just because you want it.

"Have you gone dumb?" he asked me when I still didn't say anything.

"I *am* marrying Aparajita dad. Next summer. You don't want to hear that and I don't know what else to say." If he could be calm and businesslike, so could I.

"You don't have my permission Sonu." He stood up too. We were face to face. He was as tall as I was, slightly taller.

"Then I will have to marry her without your permission dad."

He stared at me for a few seconds. "If that happens… I will neither see her face, nor yours. Go ruin yourself somewhere else."

I had to give it to him. He could say even *that* calmly.

"Sure dad. If that's what you want." I turned around and started walking away.

"Sonu?"

I stopped and turned to look at him.

"You are my only son. Don't disappoint me. Change your mind."

"I can't dad."

He shrugged. "Ok, do as you wish." He pulled his chair into position, sat down, and started working again.

Slowly and calmly, I walked out of his room to start life on my own.

Delhi, 2005

There were plenty of times when Gill Uncle grinned at me with a *I told you so* look. But I never had the chance to give it back to him. Except on the day I walked out of my house.

When I told him I had decided to leave my parents, he was aghast. He shook his head in distress: "This is all wrong. Extremely wrong." Then he turned on me. "You are an idiot! And so are they!"

I was taken aback. "Why are you shouting at me?"

"Because a parent-child relationship is sacred," he said. "You don't bloody trash it like this!"

"I didn't trash it. It's they who are refusing to accept Apu."

He told me to shut up. That whatever happened must be ninety percent my fault – I was always looking for chances to fight with my parents. "They are going to suffer ten times than you, and they don't even know it. Ask someone who has lost a child!"

I had seldom seen him so pained. So I decided to mellow down. "What do I do if they don't want to accept Apu? Leave her?"

"Have you heard of a word called *persuasion*?"

"I tried. It was impossible!"

"I don't believe you. The way you are, you would have barged in their room and tried to hammer it down their throats."

I said it was nothing like that. But if that's what he thought had happened, he was welcome to persuade my parents otherwise. If they agreed to accept Apu, I would give up my plans of leaving them that very instant.

"Really?"

"Try me."

"Ok."

Saying he was more than ready to take up that challenge, Gill Uncle immediately walked off to meet my parents. But when he returned after an hour or so, he was much somber. He didn't meet my eyes. Looking down, he slumped on the sofa and began fiddling with the wooden paperweight.

"What happened?" I asked.

… … … … … … …

"What happened Gill Uncle?"

"You father refused to meet me. And your mother threw me out of the house."

"What?"

How could they? I mean he was *the* most well-known and respected person in the colony.

"Someone told them Apu was a regular visitor to my home," he said.

"So?" I asked, even though I could guess what was coming.

"So your mother accused me of leading you astray."

Later my sister told me that was not all. The blame was accompanied by a deeper insult. Maa had not only accused him of leading me astray, she had also shouted at him that because he didn't have a child of his own, he had plotted to snatch her son away. That he had been pursuing that hidden motive since I was a kid and had turned me against my parents. Gill Uncle had spared me those ugly parts.

Why wasn't I surprised? I had expected something along these lines, only much less insulting.

"I am sorry," I told him.

"Don't be." He finally looked up. "I deserve what your mother told me."

"What crap!"

It was rude to say that. But I needed to, so I could get him out of his self-recrimination mood. I think maa's words had affected him strongly.

"No, it's not crap!" he replied. "Whatever said and done, they're losing you. She's a mother, a wounded mother."

"Well… that's *their* fault. Not yours, not mine. They could have easily *not* lost me! I was also not very eager to get on the streets!"

I didn't tell him I was even less eager now that I had actually walked out of my house. The reality had hit hard. I really had no home!

"What streets?"

Hmm… seemed Maa's word had also made him forgetful. "I don't have a home Gill Uncle!" I reminded him. Rehne ko ghar nahin… sone ko bistar nahin…? Wasn't that called being on the streets?

I got a what-the-hell-you-talking-about look from him. And was told not to be needlessly dramatic. "Who said you don't have a home? This is also your home."

I had expected he would say that. So sweet of him, Gill Uncle of mine. But I was ready to refuse his offer and tell him my Plan-B.

Delhi, 2005

"No! You can't do that!" Gill Uncle bellowed when he heard my plan. I had told him I was going to sell my Triumph to fund my homeless days. It was a decision I made the night I had talked to Rohan, mulling over what I would really do if I had to leave my home.

I could have taken up a part-time job, but it would affect my studies. Now that I had to find a good full-time job by the time I graduated, I didn't want to take that risk - I was the topper of my class and I wanted to continue in that position. So I dropped the idea.

I needed money though. Not tons of it, but enough to get by. Kapda

I had, but for the other basics – roti, makan, transport, phone bill… If you had a sweetheart who didn't live next to you or at least studied in the same college, transport and phone bill also counted among the basics.

That's when I had decided to sell my Triumph if worst came to worst. I knew a friend, Sajal, who admired my baby besides being rich enough to not mind shelling a couple of lakhs for it. He already had three bikes and I was sure he would jump at the chance to get a fourth one dirt cheap. Especially a bike of the caliber of my Triumph.

The news upset Gill Uncle. Guess he hadn't got down to the nitty-gritty of what leaving my home really meant for me. "Don't you love your bikes?" he exclaimed trying to dissuade me from my plan.

Ya… I did. But I had to get used to living without them. They were the playthings of the rich, and I wasn't rich anymore.

I told Uncle I could do without them.

"I will sacrifice one love for the other," I said grinning. "Machines for the human."

"Oho!" What a sacrifice! Gill Uncle returned grinning back. "Won't Apu be *thrilled* to hear of it?" he mocked me.

Crud! He was right. More likely I would get from Apu an extended lecture on fighting pointlessly with my parents. Out of that very fear, I had postponed telling her about the battle.

"Totally," I said. "Especially when she finds out further outings with me will involve DTC buses instead of joy rides."

Apu loved riding with me. Rather 'loved' was a lesser word - I remembered the whoops of joy she gave from time to time as we cavorted on Delhi roads. I would miss those whoops. If I had few regrets in giving up my bikes, this was one of them.

"I don't think she would care about the difference," said Gill Uncle.

He didn't know about Apu's whoops. "Anyway, you still have your Ducati," he said talking about my other bike.

"Ducati? No, I don't."

Gill Uncle gave me a surprised look and asked me why - was I selling the Ducati too? Why I needed so much money for 9-10 months? "I will get you a job as soon as you graduate," he promised me.

He hadn't understood what I meant.

"Gill Uncle," I told him. "I am not *selling* the Ducati. I am not taking it *at all*. It's not mine."

"Huh?"

"It belongs to my parents. I can't take it."

"Does it now?" He crimped his brows and settled back on the sofa, his arms around a cushion. "I thought even the Triumph belonged to your parents then. But aren't you coolly selling it? Then why leave the Ducati? What's wrong with it?"

"Nothing's wrong with it Gill Uncle!" I said in exasperation.

Then I explained to him he was right about the Triumph – like the Ducati, it wasn't mine. I was just borrowing it from my parents for a while. I would return them the money soon as I had earned enough.

Gill Uncle gazed at me with a mildly surprised look on his face. As if he had discovered something new about me. Something unexpected.

"You are *that* serious about it?" he asked.

"About what?"

"Not taking anything from your parents. Returning the money and all?"

"Yes," I said, feeling proud. I would not let myself be beholden to my parents in anyway. I would be *truly* independent.

He nodded and picked up his glasses from the table. He blew into them. Then he put them back on the table. "Not good..." he said shaking his head, "... not good." He was staring at the table.

"What?"

He raised his head looking worried. "That seriousness about not being beholden or whatever. Don't feel so proud of it. Drop it."

That unsettled me. A little. He was a bloody mind-reader sometimes. "Why?"

"Otherwise you'll regret it someday boss," he said almost angrily. "That's why."

Then he put on his glasses, got up and marched out of the room. I was astonished. What happened?

Delhi, 2005

Until I found a place of my own, I needed a roof to bunk under. I could live at Gill Uncle's, but his place was too close to my home. So I chose to live in Rohan's farmhouse - in the same room in which Apu and I had spent a few memorable nights. What more could I want?

I did one more thing - I extracted a promise from Rohan he would keep his mom away from the place till I was there. That was also important. I had dreaded meeting Sheetal auntie since the day I had heavily disappointed her by confessing to her my godless state.

I dreaded the meeting still – the godless state, if anything, had become worse. Believing in a homegrown version of god, maa and dad had not even wanted to see Apu because she believed in a Roman Catholic version developed elsewhere in the world. Result? - Everyone was unhappy. What use I had for a god like that?

My perfect world obviously wouldn't have one thing: a god.

Delhi, 2005

A couple of days later, Aaru dropped in to see me. Rohan had brought her along at her request. "Give me a few minutes with my bro," she told him and sent him out of the room.

"Why?" I asked.

"I want to talk to you alone," she muttered. She sounded damn serious.

I got a little anxious. "Is everything all right?" I hesitated. "At home?"

"Yes," she said. "But what are you doing *here*? I hate you!"

… … … ??? … … …

"I thought you would at least live next door," she said. "With Gill Uncle."

She said my leaving home would not have mattered then; she would have seen me everyday. But this place? – this place was like half the world away! "Why you taking sanyas so early bro? You haven't even married your girlfriend!"

I grinned. "Because Uncle's place is like too close to home."

"So?"

"Too close for comfort Aaru," I said. "Don't want to run into dad every morning." That would be almost like being at home – even earlier, I mostly saw dad only in the mornings.

"I know," she said. "But I will *miss* you."

I tousled her hair. "I will miss you too."

She clutched my hand tousling her hair and squeezed it. "Do you have money?"

That was sudden. "Huh?"

"Gill Uncle said you don't have money to live on. So in desperation, you are selling your things and stuff."

Desperation? @#%$#@#! Gill Uncle was spreading false rumours! "I am not selling my things and stuff Aaru," I explained. "I am just selling my Triumph. That..."

"Really?" Aaru looked aghast.

"No big deal."

"But you lo...

Oh no! Not again! "Yes... I know what you will say! Don't say it. I love my Triumph. Right?" I asked her.

She nodded.

"Sure. I agree. But people also fall out of love. Don't they? I fell *out of love* with my bikes," I said. God! How many times would I have to repeat that?

I told my sister it happened the day I fell in love with Apu. Perhaps my heart was not big enough to hold three persons - rather one person and two things. And yes, my bikes were now *things* for me - *machines.* Nice beautiful machines, but machines. Could she... someone... anyone... start believing that?

"No."

"You don't believe that?"

She shook her head.

"Why?"

"Do you? Yourself?" she asked. "Sach bolna."

I was stumped by that bouncer. Did I believe? Got me thinking for a few seconds.

Honestly, Aaru was right. I wasn't quite sure.

"See," Aaru chirped. "I know you. You can't lie to me."

"Ok. But what can I do? Choices... sacrifices have to be made."

She punched my chest twice, once with each fist. "Stop maaroing filmi dialogues bro."

"I am not maaroing anything! That is the plain truth."

She pulled her bag down from her shoulder and opened it. "See. You don't need to ditch your Triumph. I have got some money." She pulled out a wad of notes and thrust them towards me. A mix of five hundred and thousand notes. There were quite a lot of notes!

When I didn't respond, she shook the bunch before me. "Hello?"

I frowned. "How did you get this Aaru?"

She shrugged. "How does that matter?"

"It does. Is it mom's?"

"No! Mine."

"Yours?" I couldn't have sounded more skeptical. "You started acting in Ekta Kapoor serials or what?"

"Don't be mean. I sold something of mine to get it," she said evasively. She was looking away.

OMG. Why? I had half a mind to shake up and down this caring, but stupid, hasty girl.

"You sold *something*! What?"

... ...

"WHAT AARU?"

"Don't shout at me Ani!" she said turning her face. "A necklace."

God! This was going from bad to worse. I itched to wring her neck.

"A necklace... And?"

"And... nothing."

"Don't fib Aaru! A necklace will not get you that much money. What else?" I said in my most authoritative voice.

"Two necklaces..." she said. I frowned at her. "And a bracelet..." I frowned some more. "And a payal." I frowned even deeper. But nothing more came out.

"You sold three neckla- !"

"No!" she exclaimed cutting me. "Total two necklaces only. And a bracelet, and payal. That's all."

"That's all!" I mimicked her. "Wow! Why couldn't you sell some more stuff? Maybe the entire set that Ma gave you for Meena didi's wedding?"

"Don't be sarcastic!" she replied getting angry. "I just wanted to help you."

I gave a wan smile. I loved her. And inside, I felt like hugging her for doing what she had done. But I couldn't. I had to scold her and disappoint her. Send her back with the money, and then later get her jewels from whoever the stupid girl had sold them to.

"You wanted to help me?" I asked. "By selling your jewels?"

"Yes."

"Great! Now who's being filmy?"

Delhi, 2005

Switching off the engine in Sajal's driveway, I just sat there for some time, hunched over my bike, holding the handlebars tight, looking through the windscreen. A street-cat sitting in a corner licked its furry leg. The wall above it looked as if someone had spilled green paint over it generously. A lightbulb was still on though it was almost ten in the morning.

No, make that two lighbulbs! Bloody wasteful people.

I didn't want to get down and call Sajal. I could have waited forever, but the watchman didn't let me. "Shall I call Sajal Bhaiya?" I heard him say from the back after about ten minutes.

"Yes," I said reluctantly. Ok, let's get this thing over with.

After he came out and greeted me, Sajal invited me inside. But I didn't want to go. Why prolong the whole thing? I made an excuse and we chatted for a couple of minutes in the driveway itself. Then he asked me if he should bring the cheque.

"Yes."

The key was ready in my hands when he came back. We exchanged – the cheque and the key. I asked him if he would like a test ride before we finished the transaction, but he refused. Said the two rides he had already taken a week before were enough.

"You'll like riding her… it," I said politely, putting the cheque in my pocket.

"I know," he said patting the seat. "It's a beauty. Don't hesitate to call me if you want to take it anytime."

That would be unlikely. "Sure. I will."

"You sure you won't come inside? We can have chilled beer. I have plenty saved from a party we had last night."

"No. Got to go."

"Ok, dude. Bye then."

"Bye."

We shook hands and I turned to go.

"How are you going btw?" Sajal called from behind.

I turned back. "In a taxi… I guess."

"Shall I drop you on the main road?" he asked gesturing at the bike.

I looked at his Triumph. She looked even more beautiful. "No. I will manage."

"Sure?"

"Yup. Quite."

I slowly walked out of the gate, walked till the main road and caught a DTC bus.

Delhi, 2005

Now that I had enough money to survive the nine-ten months before I started earning, I rented a small two-room flat in Kamala Nagar on shared basis with a classmate: Kunal Srivastav. It was pure luck. Kunal's previous flatmate had just left town and Kunal was searching for a new one. I managed to drop in just at the right time.

Kunal and I hadn't interacted much in the two years we were classmates. Rather, we hadn't interacted at all. He was a quiet, studious looking guy from Ranchi in Jharkhand. Before we became roommates, I knew just one thing about Kunal – that guys made fun of him because he had a deep crush on a junior called Chitra (they shared hometowns) and he thought the best way to impress her was to sing ghazals to her.

As expected, Chitra, in spite of actually being called Chitra Singh, hadn't responded favorably to his ghazals. Woh na thi kunal ki kismet… I guess.

Kunal turned out to be a great flatmate. He was an easy-going, sensible person, notwithstanding the Chitra chronicles. Method and hard work made him good at academics – and I needed to be with someone like that this year. Best of all, he was a romantic – he was simply floored by my love story and promised me he would make sure I had lots of time to spend with his Apu Bhabhi without him becoming the kebab mein haddi.

It was funny – the way he addressed and treated Apu. As respectfully as if Apu was old enough to be married to me for ten years. Another thing – Apu was from IIT. And people from his part of country apparently treated them with awe. Altogether, I think Apu got as much respect from him as the President got from marching soldiers on Republic Day. Perhaps more.

"Do I look that old?" Apu asked me ruefully the first day they met. We were waiting for the train at Kashmiri Gate metro station after visiting my new flat. All the time we were at the flat, Kunal had refused to call Apu anything but Bhabhi, kept starting his sentences with "aap", and stood up in attention anytime she moved. Apu was, too put it mildly, overwhelmed; I was amused.

"No. But you know what? Maybe you look scary to him."

Apu protested immediately. "I don't! Bhabhis are not scary. Not Apu bhabhi anyway."

"How do you know?"

"I know!" she exclaimed punching me on my shoulder. She threatened me that if I called her scary once more, she *will* be scary. Then she made a face. "But how do I get him to treat me like… *my age*!"

"Feed him," I advised her rubbing my shoulder - she had hit me hard. "Great food. Then you can tell him you will not feed him again unless he started calling you Apu."

"You think that will work?"

"Hundred percent meri jaan." She made heavenly food; we guys had been starving for the whole week; it was *the* perfect solution.

Apu turned towards me sharply. "You guys have been starving for the whole week? Why?"

Shit! I hadn't intended to let that out. The thing was Kunal's previous cook had resigned soon after I joined Kunal (don't ask me why) and we had not been able to find a new one. Both of us hated the only available tiffin or rather the tiffinwali aunty. So we had to choose between starving or eating out. Neither of us was flush with money, so this week we had more starved than eaten out. Anyway, now that the cat was out of the bag, I told Apu the truth: yes, we hadn't eaten well this week because our cook had ditched us.

She didn't believe me. She thought it was because I hadn't got enough money to buy even food!

"I am not *that* poor Apu!" I exclaimed.

She ignored me and began to open her handbag. I had a feeling of déjà vu. Seemed every girl around me had decided to sell her jewels to support me!

"What are you doing?"

She said she was giving me some money. She had saved about fifteen hundred from what her dad had sent her this month. I could use that to not stay hungry.

"How did you manage that?" I asked. "By scrimping on sanitary napkins?"

She was taken aback. "What?"

"If you didn't realize, I am being *nasty*," I said.

Apu didn't say anything immediately. She just stared at me with an inscrutable look.

Very soon I started feeling bad for what I had said. Really really bad. I guess I could be a real jerk sometimes. I clutched Apu's arm. "I am sorry. I shouldn't have said that. Don't know what came over me."

Apu gently removed my hand from her arm. "*I* know what came over you," she said. Then she stepped forward. We were standing close for a Delhi metro station. Quite close. "Remember how angry you were when I refused to take something from you the first time?"

The time when I tried to give her a cell phone. How could I forget it? "Yes."

"Because you said I was your girl?"

I nodded.

"Aren't you my guy?"

... ...

"Shouldn't I be equally angry now?" she went on in an even voice. Or did she have a lesser right over me just because she was a girl?

She wasn't showing it, but even I had enough EQ to know she was angry, that I had hurt her. What could I say? "It's not that Apu. I really don't need the money."

"But *I* need you to take the money."

"Why?"

"So that I know in hard times you can lean on me. That's what love is."

I understood. Perhaps my EQ increased when she was standing close to me. I smiled and put my hand out. "Ok. Give it."

She put the fifteen notes of hundred in my hand. "Thanks," she said. "I can now sleep better."

With impeccable timing, the train came rushing in. But my increased EQ told me I had to do more to make it up to her. "I am still starving," I shouted at her over the din of the metro station. "Where are you feeding me for helping you sleep better?"

"Feed you? Why? I already gave you the money sweetheart."

I grinned. "Times are really hard. I need to lean on you harder."

She grinned back. "Ok. What do you want to eat?"

Yes! "Anything... but Chinese!"

We had a fabulous dinner at Connaught Place. Indian dinner. Apu paid. Of course, there was no champagne, only coke. But trust me, even coke tastes better than champagne when paid for by a girl who you can lean on in hard times.

Delhi, 2006

The hard times didn't last. Or soon I knew they wouldn't last. In January 2006, I got the job of an analyst with an investment bank. I had prepared well for the interview. From Adam Smith to Frederic Hayek to Thomas Schelling (whom I especially liked) to Milton Friedman to Amartya Sen, I was ready to answer questions on economic theories of any goddamned giant.

But funnily, the interview wasn't on economics at all. I was asked just one, half-hearted question on Arrow's Theorem. That's it. The rest of the time, they went on and on about my mathematical knowledge.

They were impressed in the end. I could see that from their face. One of the three interviewers asked me how I knew so much mathematics that I wasn't supposed to know. I was tempted to say, "Dude, it's all because of Gill Uncle."

But in an interview, you aren't supposed to give credit to other people. So I just told them I loved mathematics – the queen of the sciences.

"Queen of the sciences! Wow!" one of them said. "Did you make that up now?"

In an interview, you aren't supposed to tell the truth either. "Yes."

That impressed them even more. I wasn't only mathematical, I was creative too. Wow! I guess their world was filled with wow!s, they uttered that word so many times.

Anyway, they lapped up my bullshit and gave me a job. One of the highest paying jobs in the entire campus. My name even got printed in the newspapers.

That day I was happy. No happy is a lesser word – I was ecstatic.

Because that day I didn't know they were going to make a noose out of that bullshit and tie it around my neck. Gill Uncle tried to warn me that I *may* not like what I was getting into, but I was in no mood to listen to anything negative. I just wanted money and baby! I had got it.

Wow!

Mumbai, Nov 27, 2008

I dreamt that Apu was lying next to me, and she giggled and pushed me away when I tried to put my arm around her. When I asked her why she said I was leaning over her even when times were good and she couldn't bear me anymore because I had become so fat from eating her excellent cooked food. I pretended to be pissed at her for calling me fat and shut her up with a kiss on the lips.

That's when her call came.

Delhi, 2006

I was feeling envious. It was Apu's convocation, the 37th one at IIT Delhi. She was dressed up in a purple robe with a red scarf around her neck or whatever they called it, trying to look all serious and scholarly. So was her entire batch - I was standing in a sea of purple IITians, all trying to look serious and scholarly.

In vain, I would say, since they were looking more like comic artists. To soothe angry IITD hearts, the purple men and women did have the potential of looking scholarly, but the rather colorful gown was diminishing the intended effect. The entire class looked as if scarfpehen-ke-phool-khila-hai. Purple waala. Or perhaps it was just the envious me trying to make fun of the august convocation because I didn't have one coming anytime soon.

Goddamned DU! What did you study for if not for a job, and equally important, a good, noisy convocation where at the end you got to hug all the pretty classmates with big boobs who you had always wanted to hug tightly but never could?

Well, I had no such pretty classmate, it was not my convocation, and I certainly didn't dare to hug Apu tightly before Jerry who was there at the convocation along with us. So green with the unfulfilled desire for a convocation and hugs, I contented myself by teasing Apu about her purple robe. And her dear friend Cheeni.

"Where's Cheeni?" I asked her looking around.

"Why?"

"Is he graduating too?"

Apu gave me *the* look. "Yes, he is. And at the top of our class."

"Really?" Even with the glasses, Cheeni hadn't looked the studious kind. To tell the truth, that's what had got me jealous in the first place.

"Yup," Apu said, her lips pursed. "Sorry, but he beat you dude."

Apu was saying that to tease me because in the end, unlike Cheeni, I hadn't graduated at the top of my class. I had sort of taken things easy after I got a job. Why work your ass off when you weren't going to study further? Ramakanth, the dude who was second in the class, had surged ahead of me in the final exam. But who cared? Or at least that's what I had kept telling Apu.

"No, Cheeni didn't beat me," I said. "I beat him where it really matters."

Apu raised her eyebrows.

"I got the prettiest girl of *his* class as *my* girl."

Apu grinned at the backhanded compliment. "Really? You don't find anyone here prettier?"

Hmm... someone was fishing for more compliments. I looked around and finally settled on a person. "Yes... I do see one."

Apu's eyes widened. "Who?"

Ha! Jealous... was she?

"Cheeni," I said. "Isn't he sweeeeeet!" Then I hit the run home. "Shit! I think I am becoming gay. Ab tera kya hoga re Apu?"

Poor Apu. In spite of the enormous temptation to give me a solid jhaap as she loudly declared, she couldn't chase me. She was heavily impeded, wearing a heavy gown in a sea of purple creatures with Jerry standing nearby.

About two and a half hours later, Apu was formally declared an electrical engineer by Azim Premji. She looked awesome as she got her degree. Just for that one moment, I also wished I were in the 37th graduating class of IIT Delhi. I guess it must feel good to have your hard work recognized by someone that distinguished.

"You are finally an engineer Apu!" I exclaimed to her when after hugging Jerry, she came waddling towards me like a penguin.

"Yeah! And you are a nut," she whispered in my ear when she was close enough. "Now I have legal permission to screw you good."

See... even having an engineer girlfriend has its good points.

Delhi, 2006

We fixed our wedding for October. I wanted to do it small - have a court marriage and a small party afterwards. But Apu refused to hear of any such thing. When I told her my plans, she put her fingers in her ear and pretended she couldn't hear me as Gill Uncle grinned from his home bar; we were at his place having dinner. "It will be one of the most important events of our life," she exclaimed after I was done. "Screw your plans! I am not going to do it *small*!"

"What do you want then?"

"I don't know. But I want at least a gorgeous wedding dress. I want to *look* like a bride!"

It turned out Apu wasn't the only one wanting a big wedding. I was heavily outnumbered on the wedding size front. From Jerry to Aaru to Rohan to Gill Uncle to Dibbs, all of them wanted a big wedding.

Yes, *even* Gill Uncle. "I want something substantial," he declared when we were discussing the matter again a couple of days later. Substantial? What did that even mean? What were we discussing – the wedding or the wedding cake?

"Since when are *you* into weddings?" I asked him.

"Not into weddings," he said. "But definitely into excuses to hold big parties at my house where wine will flow like water."

He told me it was a long time since there was a big celebration at his house. He sounded wistful, and I *so* hated to do that, but I had to remind him that having any celebration at his house, big or small, was out of the question. My parents were right next door!

He was unfazed. "So what? We will invite them also. In fact, it will be a good time for the reunion. For them to meet and bless their amazing daughter-in-law."

I didn't say anything; I didn't want to get into an argument by telling him that there would be no such reconciliation. Not now, not ever. I had managed the last ten months without my parents quite well. And if I could do that, I could manage the rest of my life in the same way, thank you very much.

Apu and I finally decided to have our big wedding in Goa. Jerry was ecstatic when he heard that, Gill Uncle not. In fact, for almost an entire week, Gill Uncle refused to talk to me pretending to be hurt. Jerry on the contrary declared it was exactly how it should be – where else a wedding took place if not at the bride's house?

Aaru, for obvious reasons, was on Gill Uncle's side; Rohan, for not so obvious reasons, was on Jerry's. Then one evening I discovered Rohan's unobvious reason for supporting a Goan wedding. "Daaru bhai daaru, sasti daaru" – my dear friend declared while under the influence of the same daaru. Bewra saala!

Deciding the wedding venue was not even ten percent of the headache. There was a bigger problem yet to be solved – to decide *how* we should get married. I knew if Apu had her way, we would spend an entire week doing nothing but getting married. She wanted to first get married in a church, then in a temple, then in a court…

I mocked her. "Why leave the Arya Samaj alone? Let's get married there too."

"Good idea!" my intended said. And I thought IIT electrical engineers were supposed to be enthu about diodes and triodes, not weddings!

"But why you want to get married in so many places?"

"So when you run away with Teena, I have lots of evidence to present in court to get you back."

"I won't run away with anyone!"

"Then I will run away with Cheeni and you can use the evidence to get *me* back."

I didn't say more.

I don't know whether to call it lucky or unlucky, but Apu finally didn't get her wish. The executives of our respective holy places didn't warm up to the idea of an inter-religious marriage happening under their dominion. I wasn't a Catholic, so we couldn't get married in a church, especially since we refused to give any undertaking that our kids will be raised as Catholics. Apu wasn't a Hindu, so a temple was out too. Anyway, marrying in a temple is pretty old-fashioned, the talkative priest of a temple we visited consoled us; maybe *modern types* like us should get married *underwater*. Later, Apu said she was happy the priest at least said modern types like us should get married – even if underwater!

We eventually got married in a court with a big Vor (wedding party) planned at Jerry's in the evening. Jerry and one of Apu's Uncles, Samuel, were the witnesses from bride's side; Gill Uncle and Rohan were from mine. Things were going almost as planned, without any hitches, when at the last moment, the witness list drew a loud protest from Aaru.

"I want to be a witness too," my sister demanded in the court grounds taking me aside. "I am your sister!"

Not the one to leave the hint of a trouble alone, Rohan had followed us. "I guessed right," he commented when he heard Aaru's demand. He smirked at her. "The witness has to be an adult Aaru."

"I *am* an adult!"

"The witness also has to *look* adult."

Aaru stiffened. Oops!

I didn't want to let the court turn into a minor battlefield between my sister and my friend, so I tried to reason with Aaru. Yes, I conceded she was just over eighteen ("and I have my passport to prove it," declared Aaru). So yes, maybe it was legally ok, ("it is," said Aaru). But surely wouldn't the officials be more comfortable if the witnesses were a *little* older?

Bloody Rohan couldn't stop his expert comments. "Not little dude. Quite older!"

Aaru flared up once again. "I have fought a big battle with maa to be here. He..." Aru said pointing at Rohan, "has done nothing!"

Frankly, they snapped at each other so much these days, I suspected there was something going on between the two of them.

"That's a lie!" exclaimed Rohan. "You haven't fought any battle. Auntie sent you here herself."

I frowned.

"Ask her," Rohan said. "Auntie has even given her the Mangalsutra that Apu is going to wear now."

I looked at Aaru. She didn't meet my eyes this time.

"Is this true?"

... ...

"AARU?"

"Yes," Apu replied hesitantly. "Maa..."

I stopped her saying I didn't want to hear more. Then I returned to continue with the wedding.

Apu looked gorgeous when, accompanied by her cousins, she arrived at the court. To give credit where it was due, she was dressed like a Sindhi bride to perfection. Someone had done some serious background research. IITians!

"You do *look* like a bride," I teased her when she came close.

"Tell me," she whispered. "I can't even keep my eyes open they are so heavy with makeup."

"Who did this to you?"

"What do you *mean* who did this to you?"

I chuckled. "I mean who did this *for* you?'

Apu first showed me one tight slap. Then she said: "Dad got me the dress. It's some designer thingie. And the makeup is Isabel's (her cousin) work. She is studying to be a beautician. I was her guinea-pig."

"Isabel is good. You look amazing."

"I know. But don't try to kiss me." She grinned. "Unless you want to break your fast with oodles of red lipstick."

I grinned back. "So what's the plan? How are we doing this?"

"It's simple," said Apu. First I would put sindoor on her head and tie the mangalsutra around her neck. Then we will exchange rings. Then we will sign on the marriage agreement and others will sign after us. And then we will be declared husband and wife unless I had already married Teena and she turned up on a ghodi to remind me of our everlasting love and we galloped away to the background music of Bollywood songs while everyone else (except for Apu of course) clapped at the jeet of saccha pyar.

"*You* are my only saccha pyar!"

"Good. Then start putting the sindoor on my head."

In spite of knowing it was not a good time, I couldn't help it. "How you got the mangalsutra Apu?"

"Dibbs got it from Delhi for me," she replied promptly. "Look how's it?" She took out the mangalsutra from the purse for me to see. It was an intricate, well-crafted and heavy piece of jewelry. Very much something like maa would buy.

Apu was lying. She knew then where the mangalsutra had really come from.

Everyone started to congregate around us once Apu took out the mangalsutra. They thought we were beginning the ceremony. Everyone except for Aaru and Rohan. I saw they were watching us from a distance, looking at us apprehensively. When our eyes met, Rohan shook his head at me, his mouth forming a wordless "please", while Aaru jerked her eyes away.

I looked around. It was not a good time to broach the topic.

I touched the Mangalsutra. "It's very beautiful," I told Apu. "Dibbs has nice taste." And I left the matter there.

Goa, 2006

I wore to the court a suit gifted to me by Apu.

When Apu had given me the suit, I had protested saying I could buy my own suit for my marriage – if she remembered, I had started working in a pretty well-paid job and was poor no more! But Apu waved my arguments away. "Let it be the last and best remembrance of the times when I was richer than you," she said. So I was going to be married in a suit given to me by my soon to be wife.

A few minutes later, that suit was sprayed red. With my incredible lucky streak, I managed to drop a teeny bit of sindoor near Apu's nose and some of those particles I guess found their way inside her nose. She sneezed hard, her head jerking forward. It hit my hand holding the sindoor dibbi, and most of the sindoor fell on my suit. Some of it filled the air too. The atmosphere was reddish for a few seconds.

"Oh! I am so sorry," cried Apu when she recovered.

I glanced around. The Additional Divisional Magistrate Mr. Padgaonkar, who was supposed to solemnize the marriage, was looking wide-eyed (he too had received some share of the sindoor), Gill Uncle and Jerry were blessing Apu saying "Cheeranjivi Bhava" and "God bless" respectively, while many other in the wedding party were laughing.

"Are you ok?" I asked Apu clutching her arm to steady her.

"Yes… and no! This is like… so *bad*," she said softly.

I didn't ask why it was so bad. There was no time. A quarter of an hour later, with rings in our fingers, mangalsutra around Apu's neck and many signatures on the marriage form, Mr. Padgaonkar declared us husband and wife.

Goa, 2006

I wore the same suit to the evening wedding party, of course with all that sindoor cleaned off it. Apu, on the other hand, was decked in a virgin-white wedding gown, looking lovely again. Well, she may not have been able to get married in many places, but she had certainly managed to look the lovely bride in many ways.

I was apparently the subject of much speculation among the wedding guests. "Everybody's asking about you," Isabel, Apu's cousin, told me while we stood together sipping our cocktails.

"Asking about me or the absence of my family?"

Isabel grinned. "Both. You are handsome. You are supposed to be very rich. And nobody can understand how come your sister is here but not your parents."

"Huh… neither can I." And by the way, I told her that I didn't know about the handsome part but I certainly was not rich. I was as poor as a mouse.

Isabel shook her head as if she didn't believe me. Then she remarked: "Apu says you don't believe in god. Is that true?"

That took me by surprise. I mean I wasn't expecting anything remotely of that kind. I mean why the question, even if it was true. Was Isabel another Sheetal auntie? "Uh… yes. Not the general kind."

"General kind?" she said taking a sip from her glass.

"I mean the kind of god… umm… you know when you pray to them, they apparently get happy and do things for you. That kind."

"You don't believe god helps us?"

"I mean I don't know. But even if he does, I certainly hope not only those who pray to him. I will not have respect for such a god, so I won't pray to him anyway."

Isabel smiled. "I think I get you. More Sangria?" she asked pointing at my glass. It was almost empty.

"No, I am good."

"Yes, you need to be. For Apu," she said winking. "So you don't believe in wedding vows either?"

"Wedding vows?" Now I didn't get her. I told her that.

Isabel raised her eyebrows. "Umm… I thought you didn't believe in wedding vows and all. I thought that's why we didn't have them even though Apu was dying to have them."

I was surprised. The information, if true, was troubling. "Nothing like that. I am quite in favor of wedding vows. How do you know Apu was dying to have them?"

Isabel was surprised too. "You don't know? It was in Apu's wish list. She told it to me the last time we talked a month ago. I was going to be the maid of honor. I don't know if she changed her mind since then."

"Really? No, I don't know about this." Why had Apu changed her mind?

"Oh!" Isabel said in a sort of happy voice. "So it wasn't because of you. I didn't hear from Apu again about the maid of honor bit, so I didn't ask her."

She thought maybe I didn't like all that, so Apu had dropped the idea. It would have been unwise to pry in that case.

I nodded. "I understand. Thanks for telling me."

"Anytime." Isabel gave me a thumbs up. "Just keep her happy." She winked again. "Especially tonight."

Goa, 2006

I thought for a while about what Isabel had told me. I had to do something, no question about it. When I was fairly sure of what I wanted, I had a small talk with Jerry and Isabel and Gill Uncle. Jerry and Gill Uncle liked what I told them. Isabel not too much, but she agreed to go along with what we planned to do.

Late into the night, when all the guests had left, I sprang a surprise on Apu. "I know you plan to run away with Cheeni."

She looked tired and didn't pick up the bait as she usually did. "Too late Ani. We are already married and it's almost three in the morning!"

"But we never promised each other to stay married forever."

Apu made a face. Guess this wasn't the best time in the day for jokes. "What happened? Got a late night STD from Teena?"

I pretended to be shocked. "Eww… STD!"

Apu frowned. Then she got it. "I meant a phone call!" she exclaimed, "Not any disease, you dirty minded unmentionable!"

I grinned. "No, I didn't get any STD. But really, we didn't take our wedding vows."

Apu stared at me. "Wedding vows? You wanted us to take vows?"

I nodded. "Aa… aan."

"But I thought you were… I mean… not keen on those. I thought you wanted to keep things simple."

So I was the real culprit after all. My never ending chatter in praise of simple weddings without show-shaa had taken its toll on Apu. "Who said I wasn't?" I asked her. "I am keen on whatever you are keen on. Anything and everything that will keep you from running away with Cheeni. Especially vows. Why didn't you tell me you wanted them so much?"

Apu grinned. "They come packaged with the church wedding. Since we weren't… Anyway, why are we talking about them now?"

"Because I want us to take them."

"Now?"

"Absolutely."

"Are you crazy? It's like three in the night! Where would you find a priest? And why would any priest agree to come anyway?"

"Who said we needed a priest?"

"Huh?"

"I'll tell you what we need. We need a bride, a groom… that's us… father of the bride, a best man, a maid of honor, a couple of bridesmaids and groomsmen, a ring bearer, a flower girl… And Gill Uncle. We have all of them."

Apu was puzzled. "Gill Uncle?"

"Yes… yes. Come fast. They are all waiting for you!" I pulled Apu by her hand to the venue behind Jerry's kitchen where Jerry, Gill Uncle, Isabel, Rohan, Aaru, Dibbs, Kunal and a few of the more enthu cousins of Apu who had agreed to keep the mock wedding a secret under the pain of Isabel and I not talking to them… *ever*… all of them waited for us.

Not long after, Isabel who was in charge, arranged everyone and everything close to as it should be. We had even the right music ready – Mendelssohn's Marche Nuptiale. Then Gill Uncle, who was *unlawfully* officiating our wedding, signaled the father of the bride to start walking and the mock ceremony began.

We all laughed when it was the time for Jerry to give Apu away.

"Who gives away the bride?" Gill Uncle asked.

To which Jerry responded with raised hand, like a sailor: "Aye, aye sir."

And Apu exclaimed in mock exasperation: "Dad, be serious! I am your daughter, not your boat!"

Apu had told me that of all the family members, Jerry was the most irreverent, trying Apu's mom's patience quite often. Perhaps three years of JNU had done its trick.

We said our wedding vows after that. I actually liked saying mine. Quite a bit. It was lovely, simple and lovely. "I, Aniruddha, take you, Aparajita, for my lawful wife, to have and to hold, from this day forward, for better or worse, for richer or poorer (Apu grinned wide at this point), in sickness and in health, till death do us part."

Then Apu said hers: "I, Aparajita, take you, Aniruddha, for my lawful husband, to have and to hold, from this day forward, for better or worse, for richer or poorer, in sickness and in health, till death do us part."

"Now you may kiss the bride!" said Gill Uncle with a flourish when Apu was done.

I eagerly stepped forward. Apu looked beautiful in her wedding gown and you could say I was waiting for this the entire evening. However before I could kiss my bride, I was stopped by a cry. "No wait!" It was Isabel. Leaving us stunned, she turned to Gill Uncle. "Mr. Gill, you haven't pronounced them husband and wife yet!"

Oops! That was *definitely* a problem. I had almost stepped back, when Apu's other cousins goaded me to ignore Isabel. "They already are Bella!" Liz shouted from the right. "Yes, go for it," yelled another from behind. "Don't listen to Bella," said a third voice.

So I did as the other cousins told me while Isabel looked on shaking her head with exasperation. I kissed Apu good with plenty of cheers and catcalls supporting me from the back. We were married, again, even if so many things were unlawful this time.

"Now you can't run away with Cheeni," I told Apu when we were alone in the bedroom. "You've said your vows. Rich or poor, sick or well, we are stuck till death do us part."

"Sure I won't," she said kissing me softly on the lips. "Just keep kissing me like that."

I swelled with pride. "I kiss good, don't I?"

"Yes," said my wife. "Much better than Cheeni."

Now *I* was too tired to take the bait.

Delhi, 2006

The tiredness continued, after a brief honeymoon in Sikkim and Bhutan paid for by Jerry and Gill Uncle. Both Apu and I were in jobs that required working late. Usually, we reached home around eight-thirty, nine - never earlier than eight. I felt tired after the long day, but Apu's situation was worse - she still had to make dinner for the two of us. I was not much of a cook, so though I assisted as much as I could, most of the burden fell on Apu's shoulders.

After watching Apu labor hard for more than a fortnight, I couldn't take it anymore when one day she slept off in the armchair itself, her dinner half-finished.

"Let's hire a cook," I suggested.

"Why? You don't like my cooking anymore?" my wife asked, her eyebrows up.

"I do. You are the best cook in the world!"

"Then?"

"It's just that I want you to sleep with *me*, not the armchair," I said grinning.

"That was like *once*!" Apu protested.

"No, but you are really tired everyday. I can see it. Both of us. Let's hire a cook unless you like cooking better than sex."

Apu sighed. "Huh… how typically male."

'Hello! Don't tell me you don't like it!"

"I love it. But… Ok, forget it. Tell me how will we manage the cook?" She reminded me that both of us had to leave home by eight in the morning.

Good point. And I had no solution for it. "Ok. Let's get a tiffin then."

"No way!" exclaimed Apu. "As a responsible married woman, I can't allow that."

Finally, we arrived at a compromise. We would order from outside half the time (luckily there were good joints nearby), and the rest of the days we would cook together as usual. "And you better learn cooking fast," I was told by Apu. "Otherwise I will sleep with the armchair."

I did, I did.

But the tiredness didn't go away, especially for Apu, though she made no mention of it. I wished I could do something for her. I wished…

Delhi, 2006

Guess what my wife did with the first salary she got after we were married?

"Poore chaalis hazaar," she said showing me the cheque the day she brought it home.

I glanced at it. "Hmm… 39450 is not poore chaalis hazaar memsaab."

Apu rolled her eyes. "Ok, Mr. Detail… it's close to chaalis hazaar. What should we do with it?"

"Why do you have to even ask?"

"Why not?"

"We have to run our home stupid!"

Apu made a face. "No, your salary is enough to run our home. Let's do something cool with this."

"Like what?"

"Umm… let's blow it away on something extravagant."

"What? No way!" I put on a mock-serious tone. "As a responsible married man, I won't allow that."

Apu threw at me the towel with which she was wiping her face. "Don't you steal my lines dude!" Then she walked close to me. "No serious. I wanted to do something different."

"Like what?"

She thought for a minute. Then she put her hands on my shoulders. "You like riding. And I haven't ridden with you for a long time. Let's get a bike."

That suspiciously sounded pre-decided. "Did you think of it right now or were you planning for it the whole week?"

Apu grinned sheepishly. "The whole week."

I put my arms around her and pulled her close. "Babe, I know you love me. But we have like… the whole house to buy first. We haven't even got a good bed. It creaks so much I sometimes fear we will wake up the neighbors."

Apu laughed. "That's not the bed stupid. That's you!"

"I am that good?"

"Or that bad… But seriously, let's buy a bike. I *so* miss riding with you!"

"Why? So you too can get behind me sometimes?" I said leering.

Apu threatened me: "Dude! If you crack one more dirty joke, you can kiss the bike goodbye. I will spend the entire money on gold jewelry."

That was a *very* credible threat. So I stopped making dirty jokes and we went to buy a bike on the weekend. I added some money of mine I had saved in the bank and we bought a blue Pulsar. It was not like what I had once, but it was good.

Apu sensed what I was thinking even as we waited in the showroom to give the down payment. "It's not like what you had, but is it ok?"

"Yes, it is," I said.

"No, it's not. Your face is totally transparent."

I sighed. "Babe, either way, we don't have much choice, do we?"

"Yes, we do. We won't buy the bike for you."

"But I thought you wanted to ride with me?"

"Dude, I am not saying we won't buy the bike. We will," my brilliant wife said. Then patting the seat, she went on: "But for *me*. My bike. My money, my bike. You can ride on my bike. We will buy yours a couple of years later when you are a big investment banker. A fancy bike for a fancy banker."

I grinned. "But what will *you* do with your bike. You don't know how to ride."

"That's not a problem. I have a biker husband. He'll teach me to ride."

"What if he doesn't?" I ribbed her.

"Oh he will!" She leaned toward me and whispered. "I'll tell him till I can ride this bike, I won't ride *him*. How's that?"

Guess how much time it took me to teach Apu how to ride a bike!

Delhi, 2007

"In physics, it takes 3 laws to explain 99% of data; in finance it takes more than 99 laws to explain about 3%." This I had read in a Harvard Business Review article, imaginatively named 'Beware of Economists Bearing Greek Symbols'. But why I needed to mention it? Because it was so goddamned true, and so goddamned relevant!

The trouble was if you did follow what the wise author had suggested in the article, I mean *bewared* of economists bearing Greek symbols, you would have to first beware of *me*. Because I was one of the perfect examples of those economists (or was I an economist? I mean anymore?) bearing nothing but Greek symbols at work. All day long. These symbols were scattered throughout the mathematical equations I worked on through the day and they made (almost) no sense to me.

Gill Uncle had once told me the reason why he loved economics, why he had pursued that one subject all his life – because that's one place, he said, you really discovered the meaning of life. Human life was a game and economics defined most of the rules by which it was played, except when love or passion lead you to break them.

Now all that philosophy seemed greek to me. Forget meaning of life, if I could find meaning in a day's work, I would be happy. Perhaps Gill Uncle had got it a little wrong. He should have said economics defined most of the rules and *woe to you* if you broke them for love or passion.

Woe to me since I had broken them for love.

Apu caught me looking dull one evening after more than an hour of travel and thinking, call it travel-thinking, had got me nowhere. It was almost half past nine by the time I reached home and slumped on the couch. (My office was in Gurgaon while we lived in Saket since Apu's office was close by.)

"What happened?" asked my wife. "You look as if you are coming from a CBI interrogation."

"What am I doing?"

She frowned at me. "As far as I can see, and unless you have avatars who move between space and time, you are sitting on the couch at home."

I made a face. "You know what I mean babe. I meant what am I doing in *life*?"

She was going towards the kitchen, but she stopped in her tracks and turned back. "Ok. This is serious. My husband's going through an early-life crisis." She came and sat close to me. "Sit down on the floor between my legs. Let me give you a good neck massage. Then we will talk about what you doing in life."

After a few minutes under Apu's hands, I felt relaxed. More upbeat. Life was not *so* miserable. Soon, life was not miserable at all. I guess the heavier questions of life get less heavy under expert hands. Laakh dukhon ki ek dawa hai...

"So what happened in the office?" my wife asked me running her hands through my hair, pulling it in ten different directions. Her fingers could work magic even while being totally heartless I tell you.

I told her nothing had happened that way. It was just that I... I didn't see the purpose of what I did. I just juggled a lot of complicated mathematics... almost like I was creating fiction. Stuff that looked very mathematical and very difficult and very learned, but that was actually... *nothing*. "Don't see how it will help anyone except make money for my company," I concluded.

Apu had a different opinion. "It helps."

"Really? Who?"

"Me," she whispered kissing my neck. "You are with me, come home to me in this quite nice house every evening (she looked around), and I get to eat with you and laugh with you and kiss you everyday. Even have sex with you on many days. That's good... help."

I grinned and turned my head to kiss her sideways. "Yes, that's good help." We kissed slowly for a long time.

I guess when you are caught up in thinking about big things, you miss the importance of the small.

After we had kissed ourselves breathless, Apu slipped down from the couch to sit beside me. "Why don't you find a new job where you *can* see the purpose?"

The kiss had made me horny. I put my hand on her breast and fondled it grinning. "Because they pay badly meri jaan. They will not be as generous with their assets like you are with me."

"Don't distract me now!" Apu scolded me and pushed my hand away. She turned towards me fully. "You know right? - I would much prefer a happy husband to a rich husband."

"Yes, I know. Huh..." I sighed. "How I wished I could be both."

Apu pretended to be surprised. "You aren't happy with me?"

I cupped her breast again. "Yes memsaab. I am. At home I am not only happy, I am in *ecstasy*."

Apu didn't remove my hand this time. "Ok, I am happy I make you *that* happy," she said smirking.

As they say, it's all in the *mind*.

Delhi, 2007

In September, Gill Uncle got a heart attack. The evening's almost regular whiskey and soda had done its job.

He was lucky. Akhtar Uncle, his man Friday, called the nearby hospital immediately (thank god!), after which he informed me. It was a Sunday, so Apu and I were at home not far off (by Delhi standards). By the time we reached the hospital, Gill Uncle was in the ICU, but out of danger.

"It's a mild one," the doctor Mr. Mehra, an old time friend of Uncle, told us. "Not much to worry about, but he needs to start taking care of his health now. Regular drinking is a big problem."

I nodded. I knew what needed to be done. Flick his bar clean, no questions. Not a single Johnny Walker would remain in his house.

When we brought Gill Uncle home (his home) three days later, Apu insisted that we had to stay at Uncle's place for a few days till he got his health back. Which was a bit difficult for me considering my parents were right next door. I replied I would be more than happy if she stayed to take care of Uncle, but she should let me go.

My wife refused to listen. "When I can stay, why can't you?" she demanded.

Hello! I That was pretty flawed logic. The main issue was my parents, who would most likely not even recognize her. As far as I could remember, they had never seen her. Or at least known her as Apu, my Apu.

But they *definitely* knew me.

So for her, staying was not a problem. For me on the other hand...

I stayed though. In worst case, I would run into dad. I was mentally prepared for that eventuality. I was sure he wouldn't acknowledge me, and I could return that gesture by being glued to my cell phone while we walked past each other. We would manage to pretend the other person didn't exist.

It was good that we stayed. Capable though Akhtar Uncle was, he was nowhere near as thorough as Apu. She made sure Gill Uncle was taken care of exactly as the doctor had advised. Plus I had plenty of time to clean up the bar. And most of all, Gill Uncle had us around him.

I was touched when he told me he missed me a lot while we were gathered around his bed on the next Sunday afternoon. "I didn't know how much I would miss you till you went away," he told me. "Did you miss me too?"

I was at a loss what to say. I mean I had never exactly thought along those lines. I mean I never had the time. I mean… I just felt bad. I couldn't lie to him either. He was Gill Uncle. So I just stared at him mutely.

Apu tried to salvage the situation after goading me hard with her eyes to say something. God she must have thought I was an idiot! "Uncle, Ani talks a lot about you," she told him. "You are the one who has taught him everything. You are the one who married us. How can we forget you?"

Gill Uncle smiled. "It's ok Apu." He said he knew the old missed the young much more than the young missed the old. It was his time to miss, not mine. Then he asked for our hands. He clutched them, laid back in the bed, and closed his eyes.

Apu turned her eyes away. Even I felt sort of miserable. I should have missed him.

And I noticed that for the first time, Gill Uncle actually looked frail. And old.

In the evening, Apu decided to go after my life while we sat in the drawing room. "Why can't we stay with him if he wants us to? He will be so happy!"

"We can't Apu. We have our own home."

"That's not our home! That's a house," Apu railed. "We decide which house will be our home. This place can be our home if we want to."

"But I don't want to!"

"Why?"

"I just don't Apu. That's it!"

If she wanted me to spell out the real reason, I wouldn't. It was not that I didn't want to stay with Gill Uncle; I would be overjoyed to. But that would never happen with my parents next door.

"You know what? Sometimes you can be really selfish," Apu said almost sadly and walked off from the room.

I kept sitting for some time where I was. I felt angry, except that there was no one to be angry with. Not Apu. Not Gill Uncle. Not even my parents. Just me?

"Huh..." I sighed after sitting there for a long time. Sometime it's the only solution you have. Anyway, I decided to say sorry to Apu even if I couldn't do what she wanted, what Gill Uncle wanted.

I found her sitting with Gill Uncle when I went searching for her. They were laughing about something. "Talk of Ani and Ani is here," Gill Uncle said as I entered the room. "You will live long. I was just telling her about you."

I looked at Apu. I expected she wouldn't meet my eyes, but she did. I was so relieved. "What were you telling her?" I asked.

"That how stubborn you were when you were small. The time when you hid under my bed for hours while we all thought you had run away."

I grinned. "Yeah... sometimes I lose my head. I..."

"We all do." It was Apu who had interrupted my half apology.

Late in the night, when Gill Uncle had slept off, I found Apu standing on our bedroom porch, leaning against the railing. She was looking at the sky, at the half moon. I walked and stood next to her. "Hey."

"Hey."

I put my hand on hers. "I am so sorry about today. I guess it *is* selfish not to stay here. I just don't know..." I trailed off.

"That's ok." She turned her face to look at me. "We are all selfish in *something*." Her eyes were understanding. She meant it.

We stood by each other, silent, just looking at the sky.

"You never thought of running away, did you?" she asked.

It was sudden, but I got what she was talking about. It was a long time back. "No."

"You just wanted to find out if they cared for you?"

I glanced at my wife, surprised. How she knew? "Yes," I smiled remembering that time when I was under Gill Uncle's bed for almost seven hours, sleeping half the time. My parents were scared to death thinking I had run away. Even the police had started searching for me. And all that drama because maa wouldn't let me go to a school outing because she was doing puja at home where I was required. I guess the puja was so that I would live very long or something.

"And what did you find?"

I didn't want to say it. "Yes, they cared for me."

Delhi, 2007

The next day when I came back from office about ten in the night, Apu wasn't there. First I thought it was one of those rare days when she would come home later than me. Then I noticed that her laptop bag lay in the drawing room. Meaning she was back. Where was she? She never went out without calling me first and telling me that she was going out. I called her, then discovered she had forgotten her cell phone in the house.

When I asked Akhtar Uncle, he told me that Apu had come back quite early, about 3 in the afternoon. She had spent some time with Gill Uncle, then gone out again about 5 pm. She had not come back since then. He had no idea where she had gone.

Would Gill Uncle know? But when I glanced in his room, I saw he was sleeping. I didn't want to wake him up, so there was no other option but to wait.

I was a little worried. It was almost ten-thirty now. I mean not that it was very late; we were used to much more late nights. It was just that Apu had never done anything like this before – disappeared without telling me where she was going. And she had forgotten to take both her handbag and mobile with her, so I couldn't even get in touch if I wanted.

So I just waited. In between, Akhtar Uncle asked me if I would like to have dinner, but I said I would have it with Apu.

I didn't have to wait for long. About half an hour later, Apu came back looking quite tired. She was wearing a saree! Though she looked beautiful, that was the third thing unusual happening that day after her going out without telling me and then leaving both her handbag and mobile at home.

Apu wore a saree only on rare occasions. The last time she had worn a saree – it was on Holi. If I was scored on a curiosity meter, I would have scored ten on ten.

"Dinner?" I asked her after she walked through the drawing room silently and sat beside me on the sofa.

"A little later," she said leaning back.

"Ok."

I leaned back too. We both sat side by side without a word for a couple of minutes.

"Won't you ask me where was I?"

"If you would like to tell me."

"I am scared you will get angry."

I sat up. Things fell in place. Her coming back home really early (she must have taken a half-day off), her meeting with Gill Uncle, her wearing a saree, her leaving handbag and mobile at home (so it was deliberate), her looking... Yes, it was not tiredness, it was disappointment.

It was not difficult to guess now where she had gone. There could be only one place.

"You planned it with Gill Uncle?"

She nodded her head from side to side. "No, it was my idea. Gill Uncle only helped me with suggestions."

'Ok, let's have dinner." I started to get up.

Apu clutched my hand. "Don't you want to know what happened?"

"I can guess. It's written all over your face."

"No!" she said shaking her head vigorously. "You've guessed wrong."

I knew what was coming. She would say something negative, then defend my parents saying it was not their fault. I was not in a mood to hear that. "Fine. Let's have dinner."

But she refused to let me go. She kept gripping my hand tightly. "Would you just sit down and listen to me?"

"I don't want to Apu! Not unless my parents have invited you to live with them. Have they?"

Apu didn't say anything.

"They haven't? Why not? Gill Uncle has. And you know what, he isn't even related to me!"

"So can we go now?" I concluded and got up when Apu still didn't say anything. I had gone about three steps when Apu finally spoke from behind. "You know who gave me the Mangalsutra that I am wearing right now? It was not Dibbs. I lied to you in the court."

I turned towards her. "I know," I said calmly aiming to take the wind out of her sails. "Maa sent it to you through Aaru."

Surprise showed in her voice. "You knew?"

"Yes."

"You never said anything."

"Would you have wanted me to?"

… … … … … … … … … … …

"Can we have dinner now?"

"Your mom gave these to me today," Apu replied tangentially. After I asked "what", I realized she was showing me her wrists. She was wearing what looked like gold bangles. "We sat together for almost five hours. Chatted, made halwa, ate together, went through your photographs, she told me-"

"Apu, I don't want to hear what you and maa did!" I interrupted almost fiercely. I was beginning to get uncomfortable. Why couldn't Apu stop?

"She was crying when I left her," Apu went on as if she was deaf.

"APU!"

"She loves you and…"

I simply walked out of the room, went to the dinner table and sat down. I expected Apu would follow me shortly and then I could say sorry. But when she didn't turn up after even quarter of an hour, I had no choice but to go back to the drawing room. I found her sitting quietly, head bowed.

"Apu," I called to her softly, but she didn't move. I sat down beside her. Then I noticed there were tears on her face.

I clutched her hand. "Apu, I didn't -"

"You know I was at school when mom died. She went in the afternoon to the sea and never returned. I waited for her through the evening, through the night, the next day, the next to next… Dad kept telling me she will be found and I believed him. Then one day, six seven days later, I finally knew he was lying." Apu sobbed once. "It was not a good day."

I pulled her into my arms tight.

"Don't do this. You don't know what it's like to lose your mom."

How could I tell her it was different in my case? I mean I was not going to lose maa. She was right there. I could talk to her whenever I wanted; I just *wouldn't* till my parents accepted Apu.

And anyway, I didn't feel my parents cared so much about losing me. Maybe when I was a kid, because I was too cute. Ok, that was silly, but truly they hadn't bothered a bit when I walked out of the house. I mean I had never imagined they would let me go so easily.

But I couldn't explain that to Apu in her emotional state. So I didn't.

Delhi, Jan 2008

I was sure that the world was going to get a major financial shock very soon and it had no clue about it. Or at least most people didn't. A few economists like Nouriel Roubini or Nassem Taleb had given warnings, but nobody was listening. In contrast, our sensex was behaving like a drunken loudmouth and you know what, everybody was glued.

I guess greed doesn't only make you blind, but deaf, dumb, and an idiot. I mean to figure out that something was wrong you didn't need rocket science, not even calculus, plain basic eighth grade math would do. Couldn't someone just plot a simple graph? From 1990 to 2005, except for a few ups and downs, the sensex had climbed steadily with an average growth rate of 13-14%.

Then, all of a sudden, it looked like someone had given it a growth tonic you read about only in fairy tales. Zoom! The growth rate between early 2006 and 2008 was more than forty percent! Straight from ten thousand to twenty-one thousand!

What was going on? Magic surely!

I had told this to a few colleagues in the office, I mean the few I could trust to keep something to themselves, but nobody was listening to me. One day I caught Nutan - she was one of the saner persons around - and asked her to sit down and just think... think for a minute. The economy was growing at 9-10%. Add to that the right expectation that we were really going to do well in the future, and we were at 11-12%. Add to that all the money that was pouring in from foreign investors and you could push the sensex growth up to 14-15%. Finally add to that all the feel good factor that you got like maybe from Rajshri movies? ... and you could aaa... with teeth clenched stretch yourself on tiptoes to 17-18... maximum 20%?

But forty percent? I mean forty goddamned percent which was like more than twice the maximum expected rate?

Not only Alice was in wonderland I tell you. Even our financial pundits were.

But Nutan shook her head. "You think too much," she said, smiling.

I was a nut as always. The guy who *thought* he knew too much.

Delhi, Feb 2008

The day my firm promoted me to an Associate, I called Apu first. But she was in a meeting. Even Gill Uncle wasn't picking up the phone. So I dialed Rohan. Recently, he had shifted to Mumbai to develop relationships for his dad's business.

I had pretended to be surprised when he told me he was shifting to Mumbai. "Since when your dad got into the nightclub business dude?" I asked him.

He was confused. "Nightclub?"

"Of all the people, your dad is asking *you* to develop relationships?" I ribbed him.

"Kamine! I work even more than you these days," Rohan retorted. "Dad's set a target of growing by at least thirty percent every year and my ass is on fire."

So with his ass on fire, my best friend had shifted to Mumbai leaving me feeling alone where male bonding was concerned. However, he flew down frequently, especially on weekends, so things were not so bad. Anyway, Apu said she was there to help me with all that I may miss because of Rohan's absence: she was going to learn baski-wrestling (a new form of sport which was apparently less basketball-more wrestling, and which is what we played according to her), drinking like a blue whale, trying our best to commit suicide on a bike, ogling hot chicks and aunties, and last but not the least, bitching about each other's wife and girlfriend.

That was unfair! "Hey!" I protested. "I never bitch about you to

Rohan. Or to anybody. And Rohan can't bitch about Aaru either. He knows I will kill him."

I had been right about Rohan and Aaru – there was quite a thing going on between the two of them. Their relationship had started a little before my marriage. It was alright with me except for posing one obvious danger to my sanity. So I had allowed it on a pre-condition: I wasn't going to play mediator between them no matter what happened; they must keep all their ladna-jhagadna-jhagad-ke-akadna to themselves.

They had agreed, and I happily thought the danger was taken care of. But I forgot a couple of things: how close a friendship had developed between my sister and my wife, and how much women love to share their love-life woes with their close friends. Whether I wanted or not, I was kept up-to-date on their skirmishes 365 days a year by my wife. For example, I knew that since he had left Delhi, Rohan was getting earfuls from my sister who was missing him badly.

"What's up dude?" I asked Rohan when he picked up the phone.

He sighed sounding tired. "Nothing much dude. Work, work, work."

"No nightclubs?"

"Yeah, of course," he said in a sarcastic tone. "I club nightly *and* daily with my sales managers. Very exciting."

"An angry girlfriend?" I couldn't help ribbing him.

That got him. "Don't start! You know I am even thinking of giving Aaru a job here as soon as she graduates!"

I chuckled. "Really? What will you do with a philosopher dude?" Aaru had decided to graduate in philosophy from Miranda House, god knows why.

"Make her philosophize instead of biting off my head. Leave me in peace. That will *definitely* have a positive impact on our market share and profits." Then he changed the topic. I was his girl's brother after all. "Anyway, what about Apu? How's she?"

"Doing great."

"Really?"

That was an unusual question. My ears perked up. "You heard anything different?" Sometimes Rohan gave me valuable insider information that had traveled to him via Aaru.

"Perhaps."

"Bastard, don't act so mysterious like a girl. What's it?"

"Ok! But I am telling you only because I am your best friend."

"Ok."

"And only if Aaru doesn't come to know I told you this."

"Done dude! Now *tell* me!"

Rohan then told me that while she was biting his head off a few days back, Aaru had declared all guys were alike. How? - Guys were dumb enough not to know a thing unless it was told to them point blank. Zilch intuition! For example, Rohan didn't know that Aaru was really upset when he was going to Mumbai just because she told him she was happy that his dad was giving him such a big responsibility. And I, her dear so called elder bro, had no clue that my wife wanted a kid just because Apu Bhabhi had agreed with me that it was not a good idea to start a family till we found jobs that gave us work-life balance.

I swallowed. That *was* news to me. "Apu wants a kid?"

"Apparently. Aaru is not likely to be wrong."

I sighed. Life seemed difficult sometimes. What could I do? Unless Apu left her job, having a kid would result in her working more than prisoners of war of Nazi camps. I didn't want that. As it is, I felt guilty half the time.

But today was my lucky day. When I shared this with Rohan, he did something for which I could have hugged him if he was physically there. "Tell me," he asked, "can you spare like 8k for a good maid every month?" He then explained this was a maid who would stay from morning till night and do everything for you – from cooking to cleaning to washing… basically everything. He knew a guy who provided skilled maids like those.

Neki aur pooch pooch? I said of course I could! I just got promoted to an Associate. My company was now going to pay me three lakhs more every year. Which was like twenty-five thousand more every month! I could pay that much or even more to make things easier for Apu.

Rohan congratulated me first, then said it was a done deal; he would connect me immediately to the right guy. In about ten thousand per month, I could have Apu all to myself when she was home.

"Thanks dude! I can't tell you how grateful I am!" I gushed to him.

"Anyday dude! Just help me with Aaru. Convince her long-distances are good for relationships! Judai se pyar badhta hai. Save my company!"

I grinned.

Delhi, Feb 2008

In the evening, I left office two hours early and rushed home to Apu. I hadn't told her about my promotion yet.

"You' re early?" she asked happily surprised when I reached home.

"Yes. I was feeling unusually horny today," I said pulling her in my arms.

"Hands off! I have to make dinner first."

"Let's order na," I said trying to kiss her determinedly.

Apu grinned, but dodged my lips equally determinedly: "If you have forgotten sweetheart, today is a *ghar ka khana* day."

"But today is also a special day. Auspicious." I finally found her lips.

Mmm… We had a long kiss. "Why?"

I whispered in her ear. "I read if you do *it* twice today, you get a great kid."

She frowned and pushed me back. "Since when you started wanting a kid? I thought you didn't… I mean right now."

Hmm! Rohan was right.

"Since… Ok guess what happened at office today?"

She drew back slowly as if taking a careful look. "You look very… happy." She bit her lip. "They fired you?"

"Guess again, you optimistic bitch!"

"I *am* optimistic," she said clutching my hand. "If I was pessimistic, I would have said they hired an assassin to tapkao you, the way you go on about them every other night."

I stuck my tongue out and told her I was very thankful for her quick and incisive judgment, but I was more valued and wanted than she thought I was. I had got promoted to Associate. Now let's see who would talk?

"Promoted?" Apu pretended to be astonished. "For what?"

I grinned. "To make my wife pregnant."

"Really?"

"Uh… uh."

"Why the change of mind?"

I thought for a second. "I guess I am now rich enough to take care of a wife and a kid and yet make sure she works less than a prisoner of war."

"Ok." Apu turned and started to walk away.

"Where are you going?"

... ...

"Apu?"

Yet there was no reply from her. Apu walked into the bedroom and closed the door. I was confused. A little scared too. Hello? What happened? Didn't she want a kid anymore?

But a minute later my wife opened the door - without a single piece of thread on her body and with a naughty grin on her lips. She stood there hand on hips, in an X-rated pose. I swallowed.

"Did you order food?" Apu asked coolly.

"Uh...

"Order quick if you haven't. I can't cook tonight. I will be very busy with my husband."

"Oh... ok."

"And stop ogling me like that. Don't you have office work now?"

I was still in haze. "Office work?"

"Mr. Associate, I thought you said you were promoted to make me pregnant. Can we start the work?"

I did, I did.

Delhi, July 2008

Our first car. A shiny, new *i*-10.

I first thought it was all Shahrukh Khan's fault. I had wanted another car, a bigger one, but Apu over-ruled like me a queen. "Who's pregnant?" she asked.

"You. But..."

"What but?" she bullied me.

"Why do you get to choose a car just because you are pregnant?"

"Simple! It makes you a better car-chooser."

My… was that confident!

"Sez who?"

"Sez the pregnant girl. You want to know how? - get pregnant."

Wasn't this like hitting below the belt… or rather *on* the belt?

"How can I?" I protested. "I am a guy!"

"*That's* why you don't get to choose a car."

Well, whether pregnancy made you a better car-chooser or not, it certainly made you dictatorial *and* sexist!

"Ok, tell me at least why *i*-10?"

"Sez Shahrukh Khan… on tv," my wife said. "And it's a gift for me anyway."

"But…"

"No ifs and buts sweety! I am pregnant. Illogically logical. So shut up."

I did.

Later I learnt behind all the "I am pregnant" drama was an excel file on Apu's laptop. WCTC.xls. WCTC translated to 'Which car to choose'. In that file, more than ten cars were assessed on eight parameters that had individual weightages. Illogically logical mera sar aur mera pair!

"What's this?" I asked my supposedly illogically logical wife when I chanced upon it.

"That's… that's…

"Ahan?"

She grinned sheepishly. There was nothing to say actually. And I was khali-peeli blaming Shahrukh Khan.

Delhi, Sep 2008

The financial world waited anxiously for what would happen. Would the US Govt. bail out Lehmann Brothers? Everyone in my office was praying for it. Except for me; I knew what was coming, bail or no bail. Praying is never a solution to arrogant and collective stupidity, any stupidity.

Anyway, the US Govt. didn't answer to anyone's prayers. Lehmann Brothers collapsed on Sep 14, triggering the worst financial crisis of recent times.

Delhi, Oct 2008

I was going to be fired. The Indian operation of my company was in doldrums, three of my colleagues had already been hinted to look for jobs, and I was sure soon it would be my turn. My wife was four months pregnant, we were burdened with loans, and I was going to be fired. Wow!

I was lucky we had not bought a fancy home on top. Knowing I would be a dad in some time, I wanted to do that three months ago. But Apu had stopped me - it was not a good time to buy a home she said. Even I knew it was not a good time from a financial viewpoint; I guess I was just too happy I was going to be a dad.

Adding to the fear was my guilt: I was a knowing party to creating the crisis that had wiped out the finances of god knows how many people. In the past year, I had worked a lot on the derivatives that had a big role in this mess. I mean I may have been a very very small cog in the wheel, but that cog was right at the center of the wheel. Now that the entire story was out in the open, I could see how guilty I was.

More clearly than I would have liked. Guilty like hell! Even worse than others. I mean most of them weren't the big picture type to understand what was really going on, or too much part of the system to believe what their instincts may have sometimes told them. Not I. I knew exactly how it must all fall apart one day, and yet I had kept my mouth shut.

And that's what was killing me. I mean I was never someone who could just say 'Mast raho masti mein, aag lage basti mein' and move on. Yet this time I had known for long that the basti was going to catch fire and I had done nothing. Nothing except for buying car and buying furniture and buying vacations and thinking of buying a house and...

Wow!

Delhi, Nov 23, 2008

Nutan, my colleague and best friend in the office, put in her papers. And I didn't even know she was told to. When I asked her if she was doing this on her own, she told me she wasn't crazy. "Why would I do that? There are no jobs out there Aniruddh. There is nowhere better to go to! Forget better, there is *nowhere* to go to."

"They fired you?"

She jerked as if I had hit her. Oops! I was a total dimwit sometimes. "Sorry," I said lamely.

A lop sided smile appeared on her face. "It's ok. That's the truth anyway," she answered without looking at me. "Yep. Got fired into the no jobs land."

"Have you searched properly?"

"Almost two months now. Nothing."

"So?"

She shrugged with a wan smile. "I guess Vaibhav (her husband) will have to take care of me for now. Can't help it."

I came back to my seat feeling shit scared. Nutan was IIM and all and even she… I was most likely next in the line. And what could I say? My wife will take care of me? My pregnant wife of almost five months?

"Why don't you talk to Gill Uncle once?" Apu prodded in the evening. She had seen me gloomy and burrowed out the reason why.

"I will… Soon."

I really didn't want to. Ok, when the worst came, perhaps yes. But why ask him before that? And what could he do anyway? I mean everywhere people were being shown the door right? Even the hotshots. Unless it was pure charity, why would anyone be taken at such a time?

I tried to change the topic. "What's Kanak made for dinner?"

Kanak was the maid we had hired for eight thousand bucks a month. I looked at Apu. She looked good, rested. If not for a grouchy husband – happy. No matter how, even if worst came to happen, I had to find a way to keep Kanak.

"Aaloo – mutter, pulao and raita," my wife answered.

"Great! Shall we hog?"

Apu put her hand on my arm. "You know you can still lean on me right?"

I sighed. "I know."

But how many times Apu? And I was not your husband then. And you were not carrying our child. Am I not supposed to take care of you both?

The irony was I couldn't even say I wish I was born rich. I was, wasn't I? So what should have I wished for now? Better parents… perhaps?

Delhi, Nov 25, 2008

I took a few hours off and came home early. I just didn't feel like working after I found out it was the last day of Manjeet, a dude who worked two cubicles away from me. It was almost as if mera number kab aayega? Normally I called Apu the few times I had bunked work, but not today – I didn't want to talk to anyone. At least for a while.

Apu took some time to open the door. When she saw me, she was surprised. "You're early?" Her voice didn't seem quite happy.

Did she fear the worst had happened? I smiled at her. "Don't worry, I wasn't fired. Just took a few hours off from work."

"Oh… ok."

"Won't you let me come in?"

"Yes, yes," she said moving out of the way.

Then I heard a woman's voice from the kitchen. It sounded like Aaru.

"Aaru's here?" I asked.

"Yes."

"Great."

Then I heard another voice. Definitely not Kanak's. It sounded more like…

I walked to the kitchen. I found what I had guessed - Aaru and maa were cooking together. Engrossed in the cooking, they didn't notice me. I walked a few steps back and slumped on the sofa.

Apu came and stood before me. "Ani… please. Try to be nice to maa. Please."

"How long has this been going on?"

… … … … … … … … … … … … … … …

"APU?"

Before my wife could answer that, Aaru piped from the kitchen. "Who is it Bhabhi?"

Apu gazed at me with a pleading look for a few seconds, then walked into the kitchen. I felt furious. How long had this been going on?

I mean one day you don't bat an eyelid while your son is on the streets, don't even want to see the face of the girl who your son loves, don't come to their marriage, don't care what they are going through, whether they are happy or sad, sick or well, live or die. Nothing. And then some other day suddenly everything is fine. Rosy. Hum saath saath hain. It's bonding time baby! Let's cook together! Balle balle!

I didn't get it. Rather I didn't *want* to get it. Yet I didn't want to make a scene, so I dropped my bag on the couch and left the house. Let me get some air in the park.

When I returned home after almost two hours, I found the door open, almost ajar. I closed it and walked inside. Apu was sitting on the couch, twisting and untwisting her hair around her finger. Without saying anything, I sat down on the recliner next to her. Then I couldn't find the damn remote.

"Where's the remote?" I asked my wife.

"Where were you?"

"On a walk. Where's the remote?"

"Walk's over?" There was a hint of bitterness in her voice.

I was in no mood to take panga. "Yes. Now can I have the remote please?"

"Couldn't wait for two minutes to say hi?"

"I don't want to talk about this Apu!" I snapped at her at last. "Just give me the remote."

She didn't raise her voice like I almost expected she would. Unhurriedly, she gave me the remote. "But I do want to talk about this," she said firmly. "You insulted maa today… even Aaru. I don't understand you Ani. Never seen you like this. What happened?"

I flared up. Perhaps it was the truth in her words that rankled me to the core. Yes, I was not like this. This was not me. I hated myself for this. But who was responsible? Who?

"You want to talk about this?"

"Yes."

"So you want to talk about this." I sat up. "Ok, let's talk! Why did you invite maa?" I yelled at her.

She took that coolly. "She's my mother-in-law. Almost like my mother. Why wouldn't I?"

"Oh, she's your mother-in-law. I see."

That certainly made sense. Why couldn't Apu call her mother-in-law for some nice bonding time? Very reasonable. I had just one question for madam. Shouldn't be there some quid pro quo? I mean how many times *she* was invited to her mother-in-law's two storied luxurious bungalow? She - the loyal, caring daughter-in-law. Hundred times? Ten times? Five? *One* bloody time?

No. Not once. Unless my memory failed me, the only time she had been to that house, she was there *uninvited.*

And did she know the first time I told her dear mother-in-law I wanted to marry her, what happened? - Maa didn't even ask her name. Did she know why? Because she was a Christian!

"Does maa know your name *now*?" I went on sarcastically. "Or does she call you *the Christian*?"

"Ani stop!" Apu hissed. I stopped. There was a small pause. "How can you talk about your mom like that?"

"I am just stating the truth madam. Very bitter I know, but the truth."

"No, that can't be true!" Apu cried, her eyes furious. She was finally angry, was she? It was time.

I shrugged. "Ok, live in your make-believe world then. As if I give a damn."

My wife was not done. "And even if it was true, maa has changed. She loves me now. Cares for me. For you. She wants us back."

Did she now? Could be… I knew things changed very quickly with maa. One day I was the apple of her eyes who should be made to wear every conceivable charm on earth to stay safe and happy. The next it was ok even if I was on the streets, a nobody who could starve or die for all she bloody cared.

"You know," I informed my dear wife who was showing how she could be gem of a naïve fool sometimes, "She didn't say a word to hold me back when I left home. Not *one*. Don't tell me she CARES for me! I know she bloody doesn't!"

My throat caught as I said it. I swallowed. My eyes were burning. F**k. I tried to hold back the tears that threatened to fill my eyes.

It had hurt. I mean I always knew that dad may not give much of a damn if I went away, but I never thought maa would let me go so easily. I had never thought she would let me go away *at all*. I thought I was giving an empty threat when I declared to her I was leaving home; she would raise the roof with dad and I would get what I want.

But… she had not said a word. A *word*. It had been *that* easy for her.

I don't know why it hurt so much, why I cared so much. I just did.

"How you know she didn't?"

"Huh?"

"How do you know she didn't want to hold you back when you left home? Did you ever ask her?" my wife persisted.

I ignored her and switched on the tv. It was futile arguing with her.

She grabbed my arm and pulled furiously. "Will you stop watching tv and bloody *talk* to me?"

"No!" I yelled, "I won't!" I won't because it seemed she had zero idea why maa was really here. Unless she wanted to continue living in her rainbow colored Bollywoodish world, it was time she understood her in-laws didn't give a damn about her. Or me.

"So why was she here?" Apu yelled back at my face.

I smiled. She really didn't know? She was that naïve? Or was she pretending to be that naïve because the truth hurt? I told her that.

Apu drew back her eyebrows screwed. "What truth Ani? What hurt?" She looked confused and irked.

She really *was* naïve. Frankly, I didn't want to tell her now. What was the point?

"I am waiting!"

Fine. I leaned forward and patted my wife's stomach. "Because of this." I felt bad doing that, but there wasn't an option.

"Our baby?"

I nodded.

The furrows on her forehead deepened. "So? Maa's happy she's going to become a grandma. That's like the most normal thing in the world! Why is that *bad*?"

God! Didn't Apu get it? Maa was not here because of the child we would have. I mean not the flesh and blood living baby. Maa was here for the abstract concept called *vansh*. Her lineage. That's why even a Christian daughter-in-law had become acceptable now - she was carrying the family line. It was sickening. People didn't matter, own people. Son didn't. Daughter-in-law didn't. An abstract concept did. Bloody egoists!

I explained this to my wife as quickly as I could. I wanted to get the distasteful thing out of my system. Forget it all. Forget *them* all.

But my wife wouldn't let me. "How do you know that?"

"How do I know that? How do *I*..." Was she crazy? I mean what did the question even mean. Why wouldn't I? "Let me tell you something sweetheart! I know my family. I know where I come from!"

Apu didn't reply for about thirty seconds. We just stared at each other.

"What?"

She sighed. "Nothing."

"*What* Apu?"

"You know Ani..." she nodded her head as if resigned, "... you sometimes think too much."

Think too much? I had heard that before. *I had heard that before.* And from people belonging to the set who had bloody ruined the world's financial health. They had said the same thing and ignored me when I told them what was going wrong. Made me feel like a paranoid doomsayer. And then...and then things had happened *exactly* as I thought.

And now who was going to pay the price? Me!

Yes, I thought too much. But I thought RIGHT. So f**king LISTEN to me!

Apu's words had fallen like drops of vinegar on an open wound.

"I may think too much. But I think right. So just do what I say!" I yelled at her.

"Do WHAT?"

"That lady will not enter my house again!"

Apu looked totally disgusted. "I can't believe you called your mother that."

"I will call her what I feel like!"

Only now I realize how offensive that may have sounded. Apu turned without a word and started walking away.

"Did you get what I said?"

She answered without turning. Her voice was calm. "Yes, I did. And that's *not* going to happen. She's my mother-in-law. And I am not a bitch enough to turn my mother-in-law away from her son's house."

"Then leave me," I howled at her back. "F**king go and live with maa if she is more important to you!"

"It's not a question of importance Ani. And I am not going anywhere."

I cannot be forgiven for what I did then. If I only knew… Enraged like a mindless animal, I screamed at Apu: "Then *I* am going. Do what you want!" I walked out of our home slamming the door behind me as I left.

Before I had gone down the steps and walked fifty meters from our home, Apu called. I cut the phone. She called again, I cut it again. Again, again. Again. I cut her call seven times. Then I switched my phone off.

That's when I lost her. I mean all that happened afterwards was just a series of unstoppable happenings. She had said she was not leaving and she meant it, but I dragged her out of our home by my actions and thrust her into the jaws of death. No one else was responsible. Not she, not Gill Uncle, not Dibbs, not even the men who had started the dance of death in Taj. They just happened to be there. Along the way.

It was me. Just me.

Delhi, Nov 25, 2008

For a while I roamed around in the streets aimlessly trying to calm myself down. When I felt tired, I went to nearby PVR to watch a movie. Let Apu stew. I spent the next few hours watching the latest James Bond release QOS. It was half past eleven when I came out of the movie hall.

Slowly, I ambled back to my house. I felt much better. And now, a little guilty at the way I had behaved with Apu. The way I had cut her calls. What would I say to her when I got back? I switched my phone on.

But when I reached our place, I got a shock. The door was locked. Apu had left! Where was she? It was going to be midnight!

Instantly, I called her. But this time, *her* phone was switched off.

Where could she have gone? To my parent's house? Gill Uncle's? Roaming the streets like me?

I hoped not! It was almost midnight. Even Apu knew Delhi was not the safest of cities.

For a while, I waited for her, pacing up and down the balcony that overlooked the street, hoping she would return. I kept calling her, every five minutes, but her phone was continuously switched off. When the hour hand of my watch went beyond one, I couldn't wait any longer.

Gill Uncle's house was the most likely place Apu could have gone to, so I called Akhtar Uncle. He was surprised to get my call, and even more surprised when I asked him if Apu had come there. Even though

Akhtar Uncle was quite older to me - in his fifties - he called me Aniruddha Bhaiya and he called Apu 'Apu Didi'. "No, Apu Didi hasn't come here," he told me. "Shall I ask Gill Sahab?"

"No!" I almost yelled. I didn't want to alarm Gill Uncle.

I could sense Akhtar Uncle was very curious and dying to ask me what happened, but with great tact he didn't. He just said that if Apu came there, he would certainly inform me.

The next possibility was my parents' place, though if anyone had asked me even a day before, I would have said it was impossible that Apu could go there. Now I hoped to god she *had*. Before calling my sister to check, I called up two of Apu's friends whom she met now and then – Smita and Tripti. On an outside chance, hoping… But their astonished answers were in the negative. Finally I called Aaru with my heart hammering in my chest.

She was surprised and alarmed. "Bhabhi? Here? How…

I snapped at her: "Forget *how*! Just check!" Then I added: "With maa."

She was silent for a couple of seconds. Then she said: "Ok. Let me check!"

Please… please.

After about ten minutes, Aaru came back on the line. "No!"

Oh god!

Delhi, Nov 26, 2008, 4:10 AM

"Shall I go to the police?"

"You are panicking. Calm down."

How can I calm down Gill Uncle? My wife is missing in Delhi at four in the night. All because of me!

"What else can I do?"

"Panicking won't help anyway. She may have gone to Goa. You don't know."

"I checked Uncle! There are no flights to Goa now!"

"Ani, collect yourself! She could be even waiting at the airport!"

"What do I do then?"

"Just wait till the morning. We..."

"I can't!"

Gill Uncle ignored my words as if I was a petulant child. "Go to sleep. We will talk tomorrow morning."

Sleep? *Sleep*? Sometime around six in the morning, all the same, I dozed off sitting on the couch waiting for Apu to give me some sign she was ok.

I was woken up by the sound of my phone ringing. It was Gill Uncle. The watch showed 8:52. Shit!

"What? Did she call... or anything?" I cried into the phone.

Gill Uncle didn't answer my question. "Come to my house," he just said.

He was reading the morning newspaper and sipping tea when I got there. I was motioned to sit. I did that, expecting him to tell me something important. But he continued reading. As if nothing was the matter! After a minute, I couldn't take it.

"Hello!"

Without taking his eyes off the newspaper, he said: "Apu's gone to Goa."

Was I relieved! At least she was safe. "She called you?"

"She left from here around six to catch the eight-fifteen flight via Mumbai."

She left from here. I mean…"When did she come here? Why didn't you call me immediately?"

Finally, Gill Uncle looked at me. "She called me around eleven last night, upset and worried to death about you. Apparently, you were angry, missing and your phone was switched off. I had Akhtar pick her up and bring her here. Heard her story. Then persuaded her to go to Goa for a break early this morning. For a few days."

"Persuaded her to go to Goa?"

"Yes, I did that. I think you guys need a few days off."

What was he saying? It didn't make head or tail. "But you –"

"Yes, I lied to you yesterday," he cut me. "Akhtar lied too, I had told him to. You know," he said wagging a finger at me, "you are not the only person in the world who can switch the phone off. Or worry to death people who care about you. I thought you should at the least get a taste of your own medicine – what you dished out to Apu."

He stretched with a long yawn. Then he added with a crooked smile: "I am happy to see we weren't the only ones not sleeping through the night."

I was surprised beyond belief. "You got her here and sent her to Goa?"

"Yes."

Bloody hell! Did he know how worried was I through the night? Despite the fact that he was the closest I had to a parent, I almost had the urge to hit him!

He folded the newspaper. "Now don't sit there staring at me. Go to her, apologize and bring her back."

Furious, I got up to book the plane tickets.

Delhi, Nov 26, 2008, 11:20 AM

Gill Uncle's cell rang. He said it was Apu.

"Where's she?"

"Let me talk to her first!" he barked at me.

Pause and talk.

"*Mumbai,*" he turned his head and told me.

Pause and talk, then more live commentary for my benefit.

"*She has decided not to continue to Goa.*"

… … … … … … … … … … … … … …

"*Dibbs has invited her to freak out. Who's Dibbs?*"

"Divya. Her senior from IIT and best friend," I replied. "Dibbs came for our wedding. Remember?"

"Oh ok. She says she's going to stay with Dibbs for a couple of days."

Then their talk turned to me. Gill Uncle told Apu that I was with him, sitting next to him. That I had been here since an hour or so. And that I was doing *good.*

Good? Hello! I was *not* doing good!

Gill Uncle finished the call with the words: "No, let him call you."

Seemed Apu wanted to talk to me! But Uncle ended the call before I could ask from him the phone.

"She wanted to talk to me?" I asked him. I felt *so* happy.

He glanced up. "Yes, but I told her it's better you call her."

I was reaching for my cell when he interrupted. "Not now dude!"

"Why?"

"If you are about to say sorry to her which I know you will, do it face to face when you reach Mumbai. This is your first big fight. Make it an affair to remember."

"The fight?"

"No, you idiot!" he bellowed in exasperation. "The making up! Get her at least a hundred roses!"

I grinned. "I got that Uncle."

He was another dramabaaz romantic. Anyway, what he said made sense. I got up to cancel my direct flight to Goa and book one for Mumbai.

Delhi, Nov 26, 2008, 6:43 PM

I boarded the flight to Mumbai. And somewhere in the Arabian sea near Mumbai, THEY boarded inflatable speedboats and sped to Colaba.

Mumbai, Nov 26, 2008, 8:22 PM

I wanted to know how angry she was. But it was difficult to make that out from her voice. So after telling her I had landed, I just asked her where we could meet.

"I can't meet..."

My heart stopped. "Apu, I am-"

"Got you!" my wife interrupted me with a giggle.

I was relieved like hell. She was giggling. Things were all right.

Apu explained she wasn't angry, but she had promised Dibbs a sizzling girl's night out. That's the reason we couldn't meet. "We hit Taj at 10. Begin with my favorite - Chinese starters in Golden Dragon," she chirped. "Yummm… Then we move onto a pub called Indigo… The itinerary… Dibbs has kept rest of it secret… continues till 4:30

in the morning. *Aage aage dekho, hota hai kya* types."

I tried to cajole her. "Shall I come babe? I know some excellent Chinese places in Colaba."

"No sweety, not tonight," she said. "No guys allowed. We will paint the town Chinese later."

"When do we meet then?" I asked plaintively.

"Jaaneman!" she said. "Tomorrow only… post hangover. Till then, sorry to say, khuda hafiz."

I was alarmed. "Hello! You aren't allowed to drink in your condition!"

She laughed. "I know I know. Just taking your case."

I grinned on the phone. She sounded totally charged up about this girl's nite out with Dibbs. "Okie… tc then."

"You too," she said. "By the way, are you bunking with Rohan?"

"Yes."

"Shit! Don't dump me for him sweety. I will certainly meet you tomorrow."

This was great; she seemed to be back in her high spirits. My mom must have worked her astrological magic on the planets. Tomorrow, November 27th, hopefully would be a good day for the two of us.

I looked at the watch. It showed 8:25 pm. Rohan would be here anytime to pick me up.

Mumbai, Nov 26, 2008, 8:50 PM

Rohan came to pick me up with a big grin on his face. "So we are free tonight for a men's night out? Are we?"

"I guess so."

"You don't sound very happy at the idea. You know - it's not good to remember best friends only when wifey's ditched you."

I grinned. "What has Aaru told you?"

He threw his hands up in the air. "Nothing… nothing. I swear I am clean!"

As if I would have believed him. "Where are we going?"

"First to my apartment. Peddar Road," he said snatching my bag from my hand. We started walking toward the parking. "Should take about eighty-ninety minutes. Seventy if we are lucky. Get ready there. Phir aapki marzi. Aur khuda ki."

"Meri marzi? Can we just booze at home? Not really in a mood to go out. Sleepy actually. Not slept properly last night."

Rohan grinned a *I-know-it-all* grin. "Sure."

Bastard!

Mumbai, Nov 26, 2008, 10:03 PM

We were on Western Express close to Parel when I got an SMS from Apu: "At Taj with Dibbs. Smethin happend. Exciting. Tell u soon. Dibbs says hello."

"Why are you grinning?" Rohan asked me after I read it.

"Something's happened with Apu," I told him. "She says it's exciting."

"What?"

"Don't know. She's at Taj. Must have won a prize or something."

"Taj?"

"Uh… uh."

Mumbai, Nov 26, 2008, 10:22 PM

Rohan got a call. He didn't pick it up as he was driving. Then right away he got an SMS. He glanced at it, then hurriedly called someone.

"What?" he exclaimed after listening to the other person. It was a piercing "what".

Involuntarily, I started listening to the fragments of his side.

"Are you ok?"

"How many?"

"Who are they?"

"Colaba too?"

Rohan glanced at me sharply, his face tensed. "You said Apu was in Taj right?"

"Yes."

"Just a second," he told me gesturing me to wait. Then he returned to the phone. *"Just stay put where you are. Don't try to go home and stay away from the main roads. I'll call you again in five minutes."*

"Ok."

"Doesn't matter what your mother said!"

"Yes! I know. But just stay where you are. Just stay."

Then he turned to me. "What did Apu message you?"

"Umm… she said something exciting had happened. Will tell me later. Why?"

"Exciting?" Rohan shook his head looking totally perplexed. "Call her *now*!"

"What happened?"

"Just call first dude! I'll tell you!"

I was surprised. Rohan was never this curt. I tried to call Apu, but the lines were busy.

I was starting to get worried. "Can't get through. Says all lines are busy. *What happened*?"

"Something's really wrong. That was Suchitra, girl from my office. She says some gun attack kind of thing happened at CST station… she catches train from there everyday. Luckily happened just before she reached. She said she also heard those guys have attacked Cama hospital and some more places."

That was disturbing. "CST? Churchgate? Isn't that close to Taj?"

"No dude! CST is not Churchgate! They are different stations. But Suchitra's saying she heard something's happened near Taj also. Separately."

I was very worried now. I tried to call Apu again. Still, all lines were busy. Then I called Dibbs. Same thing. So I messaged Apu to message me back immediately giving me update on how things were going. I didn't text any of the news I just heard; I didn't want to alarm her unnecessarily if things were alright with her.

Then I turned to Rohan. "All lines are still busy! What do we do?"

"I know. Let's get off the road and find out if anyone knows anything."

Mumbai, Nov 26, 2008, 10: 33 PM

SMS from Apu: "Me gud. Gang-war outside. Shooting and all. Broke Dibb's wine glass. But we r at safe place now. Btw, I wasn't drinking. Only Dibbs."

I turned to Rohan. "Apu says it's some gang-war going on. She's safe now."

"Gang war? At so many places together?" Rohan had parked the car and we got out. "Strange. Anyway, let's find a shop with tv. Something should be on the news."

We found one restaurant soon. There was a crowd of 12-15 people already gathered there watching the tv attentively. We went closer to have a look.

I couldn't believe what I saw. All the major channels were broadcasting it.

And THEY were everywhere. CST, Cama, Leopold, Oberoi.... TAJ.

Mumbai, Nov 26, 2008, 10:40 PM

Me to Apu: "It's not a gang-war. It's a terrorist attack! Stay where you are! And hide well."

Apu to me: "Really? Ok. Will tc. Keep me posted. Am on 1st floor wit Dibbs. Many many ppl here. Vry safe. And hotel staff is amzing. Gt us safe in no time."

Apu to me: "Also am not msging nyone but u. Don't tell dad bout this."

Me to Apu: "Jerry doesn't know?"

Apu to me: "No. Didn't tell him I was comng home. Thought wud give surprise. Promse won't tell."

Me to Apu: "Ok, won't tell."

Mumbai, Nov 26, 2008, 11:55 PM

We stood in front of Taj as Mumbai police surrounded the hotel and cordoned it off. Someone commented they were going to start firing.

"Hey! Where are you going?"

I ignored Rohan. Apu was in danger and I couldn't watch the tamasha from hundred meters away like the other hundred people.

"Aniruddha!"

I continued walking towards Taj.

Rohan grabbed me from behind. "Wait dude. Don't be mad!"

"Let me go!" I said urgently. "I can get to Apu."

"Are you crazy! No!"

Idiot! He was drawing attention towards us! I clenched my teeth, bent forward, and heaving and pushing tried to throw Rohan away. Struggling, we fell on the ground.

Just then, two policemen came running towards us with their guns raised high. Bloody…

Mumbai, Nov 26, 2008, 12:12 PM

"You could have been arrested on security grounds Mr. Hirani!" the inspector barked at me. "Do you understand?"

I didn't say anything.

He turned to Rohan. "Mr. Deol, please make sure you take your friend back to his house and let us do our job. We will try our best to rescue Ms. Hirani."

He turned to me again, this time more kindly. "We understand your anxiety Mr. Hirani. But please trust us. We are doing our best."

Mumbai, Nov 27, 2008, 12:38 AM

As we were on our way back to Rohan's house, my phone rang. Apu! My eyes burned. "Apu… apu… sweety. Can you hear me… APU?"

"Yes, I can hear you," she whispered.

"How are you?"

"How else? Crouching with everyone on the floor of the best hotel of India." Even now, I could hear a tinge of mirth in her voice. "Wow! Am I in a real thriller! We dodged bullets and grenades and all."

"Are you ok?"

"Yes. Never felt better."

I almost snapped at her for misplaced humor before remembering where and how she was. I controlled myself with effort. "Apu, don't joke now. Please baby. Are you completely fine? No wounds… nothing?"

There was a second's hesitation. Then a "yes". It was a feeble yes. She was lying.

"Don't lie! What happened? Tell the truth. Please."

Rohan, driving beside me, gestured me to calm down.

"It's not going to help Ani!" she insisted. "You will worry needlessly. I am pretty close to being fine."

"I want to know! Please. What happened?"

There was a little pause. Then Apu started in a measured voice. "It's a slight gash on the shoulder. Even smaller than the one you got when you fell of your bike at my feet, so don't worry. Don't know how I got it. Shrapnel probably. We have tied it up for now with whatever we could get."

"Is it bleeding?"

Apu laughed. "Stupid. Don't worry. I am fine. People around me and the hotel staff are very helpful. Zero worries. All I need to do is practice crouching well, and I will be home safe and sound."

Suddenly there was a loud noise in the background. My heart jumped! "APU!"

Her voice became very soft and urgent. "Baby I have to go now. Something's big exploded… and we can hear voices outside. I promise I will be safe. Don't worry. Bye baby, love you…"

"Apu… APU!" But the phone was cut.

Mumbai, Nov 27, 2008, 1:50 AM

We were glued to the tv. The dome of Taj was burning but Apu had said she was at a safe distance from the fire.

"Dude, I think your parents… Aaru should know!"

I turned my head. "What's the point? They will just get worried."

"Dude it's not necessary that…

"No Rohan!"

He sighed. "Ok. Gill Uncle then?"

"No again. He must have slept off before this started. Let him be. He has a bad heart."

Mumbai, Nov 27, 2008, 2:56 AM

I got a message. It was Apu. "Think we will b evacuated soon. Everyone's talking bout it. Heard Army's coming in. True?"

I ran to Rohan who had gone to lie on the couch in the other room. "Apu's saying army is coming and they are about to be evacuated?"

He got up. "Let me confirm."

"Yes," he said after talking to Reema, a journalist friend of his. "Army or police, she's not sure… someone is planning a rescue and going inside."

I messaged to Apu: "Yes, that's true. C u soon. Luv." Then I turned to Rohan, impatient. "Let's go!"

He didn't move. Crossing his arms, he just stood where he was.

"What?"

He shrugged. "I am not taking you with me unless you promise to keep your cool when we reach there."

I lost my cool then and there. "F**k you dude. My wife's in danger! My pregnant wife! Don't tell me to keep my cool!" I shouted at him.

Rohan was unfazed. "Sorry dude, but I am not moving unless you promise me that."

He said my getting arrested or hurt was not going to get Apu out of danger. That I wasn't a superman! "You can't do anything to rescue her man. Let Army do its job and you do yours."

"What's my job?"

"Pray."

"Are you joking?"

"No," he said nodding briskly. "Anyway, do you promise?"

I had no other choice but to say yes unless I decided to fight the car keys out of him. "Ok, I will be cool."

Mumbai, Nov 27, 2008, 3:29 AM

Apu to me: "We r in prep for evacuation. Where r u?"

Me to Apu: "Will b outside gateway in ten. B safe and c u soon. Luv u."

Apu to me: "Luv u 2. Muaaahh."

Mumbai, Nov 27, 2008, 4:12 AM

Apu to me: "Yeah! Getting out finally. Dibbs requests u 2 keep lot of rum for her. Will need it soon☺ Msg u again in 5."

Mumbai, Nov 27, 2008, 4:27 AM

We stood in front of the hotel, watching the top floor burning in a massive fire. Dozens of army, police and fire trucks crowded the place around us. Searchlights illuminated the front as firefighters attempted to rescue people from lower floors.

And fifteen minutes were already gone.

Me to Apu: "Where r u? R u out?"

Mumbai, Nov 27, 2008, 4:33 AM

Me to Apu: "Apu! Msg!!!"

Mumbai, Nov 27, 2008, 4:38 AM

I was panicking.

Me to Dibbs: "Dibbs! Wat hppned? Why isn't Apu msging? U guys ok?"

Mumbai, Nov 27, 2008, 4:47 AM

My phone rang. Apu! God! I grabbed the phone. "Apu? What happened? Where are you?"

She said something, but her voice was so low, I couldn't understand her. My heart dipped. Was someone near her? Was she hurt?

"I can't hear you. Shall I call later baby? Is everything alright?"

"No, wait!" she said speaking slightly louder. "Sorry, but there could be someone outside. Is my voice ok now?"

I was scared. Who was outside? Where was she? "I will call later babe," I said urgently. "It's ok. Just message me."

"No! Don't go!" she cried in a whisper. "Don't go...." She was weeping.

What happened? Scared to ask, I waited.

I waited.

"Dibbs..." she said sobbing.

My heart sank. "Yes?"

"Dibbs... Dibbs died." She broke down. "In my arms."

Mumbai, Nov 27, 2008, 4:50 AM

"My hands are full of blood."

She was sobbing. I didn't know what to say. My eyes burned.

"There was so much blood. Dibbs..."

I clutched the iron railing. Rohan pressed his hand on my shoulder. But I didn't need comfort. My wife needed it. I wanted to hold her. Tight. Tell her it will be ok. Tell her I will be there. Tell her...

Apu broke down again. "Dibbs wanted to talk to me so much. She grabbed me, tried to say something. But there was no sound. She died trying."

"Dude," Rohan shook me.

"Apu's crying. She..."

"I know," he said urgently. "But she can't help it. You need to pep her up and get her out of there. She's in danger!"

Yes, Rohan was right. I had to pep her up. *I had to pep her up.*

"Baby where are you?"

She sobbed. "In a room. Somewhere."

"With Dibbs?"

"Dibbs is dead. I left her. I was scared."

She was rambling. I had to get her to focus.

"Baby, where are you *now*?"

"I don't know. Somewhere... somewhere on the second floor. I..."

"How far is that from where you were?"

"Can't say. I ran here and there after leaving Dibbs' body. They were shooting. I climbed a staircase and ran through corridor. And then this room was open, so I got in."

"Where are others?"

"I don't know." She sobbed. "They all ran back after Dibbs was shot. There was lot of shooting. They called me, but I couldn't leave Dibbs. I pulled her in a room. Tried to stop the blood with my hands. But... but she died. In just a few minutes."

She had to stop grieving for Dibbs right now. "Apu..." I started to say. But suddenly she cut the phone.

Mumbai, Nov 27, 2008, 4:56 AM

Me to Apu: "Baby! Wat happned?"

Four excruciating minutes went by. Then. Apu to me: "Hrd shots. Then screms of a woman and ftsteps outside. Door lock broken. Hiding on floor next to bed. Can't talk. Only msg."

Mumbai, Nov 27, 2008, 5:25 AM

Fire was raging. People were trying to jump off the burning building.

My hurt, scared wife was hiding for her life in a dark room hundred meters from me. I waited.

Mumbai, Nov 27, 2008, 5:35 AM

Apu to me: Abhishek msgd/called many tmes. Can't bring myself 2 tell him bout Dibbs. Can u? Plz? No. 9052018013. Plz.

Abhishek was Dibbs' boyfriend.

I couldn't do it either. I gave the number to Rohan.

Mumbai, Nov 27, 2008, 5:38 AM

I heard the fragments of conversation as Rohan talked to Abhishek.

"Hi, is this Abhishek?"

"Abhishek, this is Rohan speaking, friend of Aparajita."

"I am good. Abhishek, are you with anyone else now?"

"Divya's other friends? Good."

"Abhishek, I am sorry. I have very bad news. Divya is… no more."

"Yes. She got shot about an hour ago. I am really really sorry."

There was a long silence. Then Abhishek said something.

"Yes, Apu called us. They were trying to escape when they got caught in a burst of gunfire. One of the bullets caught Dibbs in the neck. I am so sorry."

"Yes. Apu is ok till now. She is hiding. She managed to stay with Dibbs till…. Then she had to run away. We are praying for her."

"Thanks Abhishek. Dibbs was the most humorous person... We don't know how to… Will you tell her parents?"

Silence.

"Her brother?"

"Naveen?"

"Thanks Abhishek. We are really…"

"Sure. I'll be in touch about Apu."

And then, when the call was done and Abhishek had been told the girl he loved and perhaps wanted to spend the rest of his life with was dead, I imagined being him. Imagined an unknown person calling and asking me if I was Aniruddha and that he was Apu's friend and he was sorry to say that my wife…

God. Please. No.

Delhi, 2004

Apu requested me. So I went with her to the famous Sacred Heart Cathedral for a Sunday morning Mass.

She hadn't attended the Sunday Mass for ages and wanted to go. But the church was like too far off, near Connaught Place, and she didn't want to go alone. So she said she would love to have me with her! And of course, she grinned, the ride on my Triumph would be the sone pe suhaga.

"You are welcome," I said grinning back at her. "What do I have to do now?"

"What do you mean?"

"I never went before to a Sunday Mass Apu. Heard of it, but never went. Some pre-Mass training I guess would be wonderful."

But she waved me off. Said I had to just sit quietly through the Mass and bear it and nothing else was needed. I'll do fine.

I managed to clear my Mass exam with a superlative GPA of 9/10 (awarded by Apu). The sterling grades were a result of my mimicking closely what Apu was doing (except for singing the prayers and attending the communion) and managing to not get into anyone's hair by the time the ceremony ended. "See... I said you would do good!" Apu said beaming at me when we came out of the place.

"Thanks!" I said, beaming wider.

We decided to have a late breakfast in Connaught Place. As we waited for our dosa and uttapam, I asked Apu if she really believed all that was said back there in the church.

"All what?"

"Umm... That you are a sinner and praying will take away all you offenses and sins and all that stuff."

She frowned. "Don't you pray something similar in a temple?"

"I don't pray," I told her proudly. "I am an atheist."

She leaned back surprised. It was like news to her. "Oh!"

"So?" I challenged her.

"So what?"

"Aren't you supposed to tell me I *shouldn't* be an atheist or something?" I asked her smirking.

She arched her eyebrows. "Am I?"

"Uh... uh."

"Maybe," she said. "But I won't. I don't pray because it's required or anything. I pray for myself. I don't mind what you do or don't."

"Really?" I was interested. "And what do you pray for... I mean like today?"

"Today? Nothing in particular. The same that I do everyday," she said shrugging, looking at the glass of water that she was rotating between her fingers. "I just feel comforted with the idea of someone up there. Someone watching over me for my good. I told god I am thankful for that."

Then she looked at me angularly. "You care about that so much? If I pray or not?"

"No! Not at all!" I exclaimed. She shouldn't get me wrong. "I was just teasing you a little. That's all."

"Really?" She curled her lips. She was amused. "So you think your atheism is better than believing?"

Well, that I did, but I wasn't about to tell her the unvarnished truth. So I just shrugged. "I don't know."

"You don't know?" She leaned forward. "Lia.... ar," she said stretching the word. "Spit it out... whatever you thinking."

"But I – "

"Ani!"

"Ok!" I told her I didn't think there was a god who watched over us or interfered in our lives to help us or anything. If you were in trouble, only people could help. Real people. You or your friends or someone. Yes... that way atheism was better. At least, it didn't give you a false hope. Things were clear – what was possible and what wasn't.

Apu didn't reply for a while. The as the waiter spread our steaming hot breakfast on the table, she shook her head. "Hope is never false you know," she said. "Just because god may help you doesn't mean you shouldn't try your best to help yourself. You should. But having that hope helps. A lot of times."

"Does it?"

She nodded, burrowing into the dosa rather vigorously.

"But what if it stops you from doing your best?" I challenged her again. "I have seen that happening."

She cocked her head. "And what if there is a time when you can't do anything to help yourself? No one you know can help you either. All you can do is sit… and wait. What gets you through then? I have also seen *that* happening."

I realized she was talking about her mom's…

A point I definitely didn't want to argue with her. Guess it was highly stupid to bring the topic up in the first place.

"Makes sense," I said nodding briskly. "Sorry if that bothered you. I didn't mean to… Coffee?"

She smiled. "To each his own." Then she leaned forward and whispered: "By the way, coffee is a bad way to get off the topic. Too transparent."

Mumbai, Nov 27, 2008, 5:45 AM

Don't know which god, where he lives, what he wants… I need your help. Just help.

I prayed.

Gracious God of majesty and awe, I seek your protection, I look for your healing, I appeal to you, the fountain of all mercy, I….

Please help Apu. Please.

Mumbai, Nov 27, 2008, 5:50 AM

Rohan told me he couldn't wait anymore. Whether I wanted or not, he was telling Aaru and Jerry and Gill Uncle what had happened. That's it.

"What's Jerry Uncle's number?" he asked.

I hesitated. What would I tell Jerry? That I had driven his daughter out of her home into the hands of terrorists? That she was on the edge of losing her life because of me?

"DUDE! WHAT'S HIS NUMBER?"

"I'll call him."

"No, you have to keep your phone disengaged for Apu!"

"Just this once," I pleaded. "I won't speak to him for more than half a minute."

Rohan hesitated for a split second. Then he agreed. "Ok. Do it fast then. And I will call Aaru."

A minute later, Jerry told me to be strong and not lose hope and that he was on his way to Mumbai.

Mumbai, Nov 27, 2008, 5:55 AM

Rohan gave his phone to me. "Your dad," he said.

I took it. "Hello!"

"Sonu bête?"

He sounded anxious. Aarushi must have…

"Yes dad?"

"Are you ok beta?"

Ok? Apu was perhaps dying… But why would he care?

"Sonu?"

"Yes dad, I am ok."

"And Aparajita?"

I almost laughed. What wouldn't I give to know?

"I don't know dad. Apu is hurt, a little, but she is alive. I know that much."

"Bête. I am so sorry. I am coming there. We are catching the next flight."

"Thanks dad."

What else?

He went on. "Everything will be fine bete. Apu will be fine. I have never even seen her. God will not let this happen." His voice caught. "I will see bahu. I know I will see bahu. You must not lose hope. You must pray. Pray to Hanuman. He is Sankatmochan. He rescued Sita from the Asuras." Dad was rushing like Rajdhani express. Very unlike him - the composed and methodical guy. Composed, even at the moment I had walked out on him. "You must pray to him. He would help bahu also. He…"

"Dad!"

"No, listen to me. Pray. *For once.* It will help. To Sankatmochan…"

He suddenly paused.

"And pray to… Jesus also. And Mary. To everyone. All gods are same. There is no difference. I am praying to everyone to save bahu."

Despite everything, I almost smiled.

"I know I will see her, give her my aashirwaad. I know they will all listen to me. I know." There was a moment's silence. Then his voice shook. "I am sorry Sonu. I should have come earlier."

Mumbai, Nov 27, 2008, 6:01 AM

"Sonu?"

"Haan maa?"

"Himmat rakhna bête."

I clenched my teeth. I can't cry. "Haan ma."

Mumbai, Nov 27, 2008, 7:17 AM

Apu to me: "Can hear heavy firing outside. U told Abhishek bout…?"

Me to Apu: "B safe sweety. Dnt move anywhere. Yes, told Abhishek."

Apu to me: "How did he take it? No, dnt tell. U know Dibbs was cracking jokes rite till she was shot."

I didn't want her to go back to thinking about Dibbs.

Me to Apu: "Sorry, but called Jerry. Had 2 tell him bout this."

Apu to me: "I knw. Dad's msgd me many tmes. He's scared but showng he's brave ☺"

Me to Apu: "Isnt same with u"☺

Apu to me: "No. I am only scared."

Me to Apu: "Dnt believe that. My Apu is nt scared. U knw? Jerry ıd maa, dad, Aaru, Gill Uncle, all r coming. We will take u home. U ıst promise to hang there."

… … … … … … … …

Me to Apu: "Apu? Promise?"

Apu to me: "Promise."

Me to Apu: "Luv u. U knw never luved nyone more."

Apu to me: "I knw. Luv u too. ☺

Mumbai, Nov 27, 2008, 9:22 AM

Apu to me: "Battry situation nt gud (: (: Shud have chrged well last eve (: (: "

Mumbai, Nov 27, 2008, 10:10 AM

Apu to me: "They flng opn the door nd fird shts in room. Think they wnt away. Dnt knw 4 sure. Am lying fce dwn on the flr. Luv u. Watver hppns luv u."

I messaged her back, but she didn't respond. Two minutes later, I messaged again. Then again. Again. Again…

Delhi, 2005

"I will ask you a question," Apu told me. "Bit strange, but you will have to answer it."

"What?"

"Don't laugh ok. I read it in a magazine two days back."

"Ok."

"It was like… if you were to stay forever in the way you died, how would you want to die?"

I frowned. "Die?"

"I know it's a little silly! Just asking. Liked the question, so…

"Ok. Let me think. Umm…

Two minutes went by. "Quick!" prodded Apu.

"Wait!" I cried. "Don't be so impatient. I am thinking of a poetic answer. Ok, I got it."

"Cool!"

I cleared my throat. "If we were to stay forever in the way we died, then I would choose to die with my head resting on the window of a bus traveling on a boulevard lined by tall eucalyptuses, listening to mozart. It would be night and there would be a cool breeze caressing my face."

I looked at her expectantly.

"Wow! That's… good!"

I knew it was good. I swelled with pride.

Now it was her turn to answer the question. "And you?"

"Me?"

I nodded. "Ya! Answer your question yourself."

She bit her lip grinning. "Simple. I would die kissing you."

Damn! Why didn't I think of that?

Mumbai, Nov 27, 2008, 10:30 AM

After twenty excruciating minutes…

Apu to me: "Srry. Door totally opn. Hrd ftsteps, so wnt undr the bed. Cudnt msg frm there. Am alive☺"

Mumbai, Nov 27, 2008, 10:45 AM

She called finally.

"Hey!" she said softly.

I was worried. Her voice could carry through the open door of her room. "Why you calling baby? Is it safe?"

"I think so."

She sounded very weak. My girl.

Till now I didn't have time to spare any thought for the men who were responsible for this, but now I felt a raging anger against them. I wanted to bloody tear them alive for making Apu suffer like this.

"Baby, let's not take chances," I cajoled her. "Let's-"

"Talk to me," she cut me. "I want to talk to you Ani."

"But baby-"

"Stop. I don't want to *die* messaging! *Talk to me*!"

I understood. "I love you," I said.

She started sobbing faintly. "I love you too."

There was a pause.

"When they flung open the door and started firing, I thought this was it. I *so* wanted to talk to you then. Once before I…

"*Apu*! *Please*. Don't talk like that baby. You will come out of there. You promised me that you will die kissing me. Remember?"

She sniffled. "Yes."

"And you have to give me our kid."

There was a pause again. Then I heard her laugh weakly. "Our kid will be hungry. Poor thing."

Yes! I had made her remember it.

"Are you hungry too?" I asked her.

She chuckled softly. "A little bit. Not much. I was in Golden Dragon with Dibbs when this thing started. She was bullying me not to eat much because the night had just begun. But I told her I was hungry and stated hogging like a pig. My nose was deep in a Peking Duck when the shooting started."

I chuckled back. "Me too. A little hungry. Ok. We will find a Peking Duck tonight and finish it for sure. No one will be able to stop us this time."

I waited for her to say something similar in reply, but she didn't.

"Apu?"

"But Dibbs won't be there."

"Apu please…

"Will I be?"

I flared up. "YES, YOU WILL BE. You will be, I will be, our kid will be. And we will all eat PEKING DUCK!"

Rohan put his hand upon my arm.

Mumbai, Nov 27, 2008, 11:08 AM

Apu to me: "Ani, my battery's gng really low."

Mumbai, Nov 27, 2008, 11:55 AM

Jerry came. We shook hands. Then he stood next to me without a word.

I looked at my watch. "She'll message in about ten minutes," I said.

He nodded. We were silent for a while.

"I know my Apu. She's my girl. Strong. She'll defeat the terrorists. She'll make it."

I looked at him. He sat bent forward, looking down at the ground, hands clutched tightly. He suddenly looked old. I reached out and gripped his arm. "I am sorry."

He turned his head. "Why?"

Why? Bitterness rose up my throat. *Safe and happy?* If only he knew.

He squeezed my hand back. "You couldn't have done anything."

I could have Jerry. Yes, I could have. She wouldn't be here if I would have. She would be safe and happy.

"She'll make it, won't she?" This time it was a plaintive question.

I closed my stinging eyes. I don't know Jerry, I don't know.

Mumbai, Nov 27, 2008, 12:09 PM

Two bodies were being brought out. I called Apu. She answered.

Every moment I thank god.

Mumbai, Nov 27, 2008, 12:19 PM

My sister to me: "We are at the airport."

Mumbai, Nov 27, 2008, 12:23 PM

"The battery will… it will die anytime Ani," she said sobbing. "I won't be able to talk. I… I am scared. I want to talk to you. I don't want to die. Dibbs didn't do anything to anybody. Then why?" she broke down.

"Nothing will happen to you baby… *nothing*. I promise." I promised. I lied. The impotent husband.

"Yes, nothing will happen. I will *not* die." She sobbed once. "I am switching my cell off Ani. Then I… I can at least SMS from time to time. Ok. Will I?"

"Yes, baby." There was no other way.

"Ok."

"But SMS every five minutes."

"Ok."

There was a pause.

"I want to hold you Ani."

"Me too baby."

"Tight. Once even if I die."

"*Don't*," I bellowed.

Pause again.

"Where's papa?"

"Next to me. I will give the phone to him."

They talked for a minute. Then Jerry gave the phone back to me.

"Hey!" I said.

"I love you," said Apu.

"I love you too."

"I lo… Bye Ani." Beep beep. There was no time.

Mumbai, Nov 27, 2008, 12:34 AM

We saw a body brought out. Then another. Then another. Then…

Her cell was switched off. Apu… please call. Please.

We ran to see the bodies.

Mumbai, Nov 27, 2008, 12:41 AM

We were waiting for the sixth body when Apu's message came.

Apu to me: I can smell smke very strongly. Cming into the room frm corridor. Seems fire clse by."

I told this to Rohan.

"Dude," he told me. "I have talked to people. Commandoes have rescued many people from their rooms. We need to know where Apu is so we can ask them to get her out. She needs to come out and find out where she is."

"But that's so dangerous," I said plaintively.

"But that's the only way dude! And she's in great danger anyway if fire is close by. Hopefully the terrorists would have gone away because of the fire."

I messaged Apu to keep her phone switched on. Then I called her. "Baby, you need to tell us your location. Where are you?"

"Don't know."

She was coughing. Shit!

"I know baby. But you need to go out of the room quickly and find out."

"Out?"

"Yes baby."

"I am scared."

"I know baby. But we *have* to get you out. There's no other way."

There was a long pause. "Ok. I will go out and check."

After about five minutes, Apu called again. She was coughing badly. I put her on speaker phone so Rohan could hear her too.

"Apu... are you ok?"

"I saw someone in the corridor!" she cried. She sounded frightened to death.

God no! "Who?"

"Don't know. It was too dark and smokey. Couldn't see clearly." She sobbed again.

"Did that guy see you?"

"I don't know! When I saw him, I rushed madly into this room. Donno he saw me or not!" Then she sobbed loud. "There is a woman lying on the floor here. And a small kid. Dead."

Rohan interrupted her. "Apu! Listen! Rohan here. Many people have died today. You got to be strong. We have to get to you quick. Just tell us where you are?"

"I am sorry Rohan," she said plaintively. "I don't know. Couldn't see anything. And then I ran into this room. I am sorry," she wept.

Mumbai, Nov 27, 2008, 12:52 PM

Apu to me: "Thght heard smeone moving outside. Am hiding in bathroom now. Sitting below the shower. Battery's almost dead."

Mumbai, Nov 27, 2008, 12:58 PM

Apu to me: "Tired. Leaning against the wall. Wish I could sleep."

Mumbai, Nov 27, 2008, 1:01 PM

Apu to me: "Ani, my battry is gng 2 die anytme. Watever happns now, rmembr I luv u. A lot. Always. Apu."

Mumbai, Nov 27, 2008, 1:03 PM

Apu to me: "Luv u."

Apu to Jerry: "Luv u dad."

Those I thought were her last SMSes.

Mumbai, Nov 27, 2008, 1:19 PM

A body was brought out of Taj. I ran to see it. It was not Apu.

Mumbai, Nov 27, 2008, 1:27 PM

"Let me go! My wife's in there!" I shouted, straining to get away from the policemen.

They were holding me. Two of them. And a third was behind them waving his hands like a lunatic. Why couldn't they understand? Apu was in there. I had to go.

"Sir please! Sir please!" When I didn't stop struggling, they turned to Rohan. "Sir please explain to him sir! Nobody can go in."

"Ani... Dude. Listen." Rohan joined them softly.

Listen? How could I listen? Apu was going to die! Why couldn't they understand? Were they crazy? I had to go.

"Dude... Hold yourself dude." Rohan pulled me from behind.

LEAVE ME!

I couldn't shake them off. They were pulling me back. Now they had become four in number. And a fifth man was coming towards us.

"Sir, please make him understand sir. We will do our best sir to get madam out. But sir has to leave. Otherwise we will have to arrest him."

LEAVE ME!

"SIR!" The fifth policeman slapped me on the head. "We will arrest you NOW!"

Everyone was watching. Cameras swiveling. No one was doing anything. Just watching. My eyes were blurring. The bright lights were swimming in my eyes. I couldn't move. They held me tightly.

I knew then.

"Dude... Try to understand. Even the MARCOS has come." Rohan pled again. "You can't do anything. No point getting arrested. Let's go no."

... ...

"Dude?"

I left for Rohan's place without Apu. The police had ordered us to.

Mumbai, Nov 27, 2008, 2:10 PM

I, Aniruddha, take you, Aparajita, for my lawful wife, to have and to hold, from this day forward, for better or worse, for richer or poorer, in sickness and in health, till...

Till I leave you to die alone by bullets or fire while I sit quietly on a sofa, safe and warm, kilometers away.

Mumbai, Nov 27, 2008, 2:15 PM

There were hushed voices. Then they came in the room. I was looking down and saw them with the corner of my eyes.

I raised my head slowly. Didn't feel like doing it. Didn't feel like doing anything. I just wanted to sit there forever, let time freeze, not know anything more, not know what was going to happen.

Let this not end. Let Apu sit there in the bathroom. Let me sit here. Forever. I can take that god. But I can't take...

I saw dad. After a long time. He looked thinner. Worried. Maa too. No sindoor on her forehead. She had forgotten perhaps.

He came and sat beside me. Maa on the other side. They put their hands on mine.

No one spoke anything. Thank you for understanding.

Together, we waited.

Mumbai, Nov 27, 2008, 2:30 PM

Suddenly Rohan rushed into the room, followed by Aaru. He yelled, "Dude! The palm trees!"

I didn't understand him. "Palm trees?"

"Dude, don't be so blank!" he snapped at me. He turned to maa who had stood up with a start. "Sorry Auntie."

Then he turned to me again. "Aarushi was telling me that she read your palm and the lines said Apu Bhabhi couldn't die or something like that and I just remembered Apu Bhabhi telling us that there were palm trees outside her window," he spoke in one breath. Then he addressed all of us. "Remember? Early morning? When we were telling her to try to break the window and climb out and she said she couldn't because she was scared the noise could draw someone? She looked out and she could see palm trees?"

Yes! I remembered now! Apu had said that! There were palm trees outside her window! I got what Rohan was trying to tell me.

I jumped up from my chair! Both Rohan and Gill Uncle had contacts in the Taj management and we rushed to find out where the trees were.

We got to know that soon. Rohan was told by his contact that Apu was probably somewhere in the left wing, on the left arm of the U, poolside, maybe close to the resident lounge.

"Can he be more specific?" I yelled at Rohan.

But Rohan shook his head.

Mumbai, Nov 27, 2008, 2:45 PM

"Can you get me inside?" I pushed Gill Uncle. "I know you can. You must know someone in the hotel who -"

Gill Uncle shook his head. "No way! You will get hurt, could die, and I don't even mean at the hands of the terrorists!"

"What choice do I have? Let Apu die while I sit here? She could already be-"

"No! She isn't!"

We were clinging to that tiny ledge of hope. All of us.

And I was trying not to think about Apu. Act. Just act.

"Then help me. Help me get her out." I hissed staring into Gill Uncle's eyes: "If it were not for us, she wouldn't be here. *We* sent her here. You know that."

He grimaced. "I so wish I hadn't," he said gruffly.

"I am sorry, but that's the way it is." I hated myself for saying that to Uncle, for making him feel guilty, but I knew where Apu was, almost, and I had to get to her anyhow, however slim the chance that both of us would come out alive.

Anyhow.

"Can't you wait for the commandoes?" His voice was almost pleading. "They are sweeping each room."

I shook my head. "They haven't found her yet. They will go systematically, no hurry unless we tell them her specific location. It could be too late by the time they find her. If Apu is alive, every second is…" I looked down. Then up again. I had never felt so sure about something. "I can't wait."

After hesitating for a few seconds, Gill Uncle nodded. "I know someone."

"Great!"

"But please don't get arrested or shot. You are already marked in the eyes of police."

I nodded. I had to stay unharmed, if only for Apu. "And don't tell anyone else about this," I reminded him. "Especially not maa and dad… and Aaru… and-."

"Rohan?"

I deliberated for a second. "Ok, tell Rohan. But only when I am in. He would kill me anyway if he discovered later I didn't tell him."

Despite our grim situation, Gill Uncle almost smiled.

Mumbai, Nov 27, 2008, 3:32 PM

We were across the road. Ten meters away was the North Court entrance, the entrance on the rear side of the hotel that some of the terrorists had used to enter the hotel last night. Luckily, the entire rear side - pool and lounge and all - was empty and silent, except for an occasional human figure running across the area. This was in marked contrast to the front side where most of the action was.

"Don't imagine this is what it is. This is misleading," Mr. Adhikari, Gill Uncle's friend, warned us. "There could be snipers on the windows."

Gill Uncle turned and gave me a significant look. I shrugged. What other options did we have? None.

Gill Uncle sighed. "Ok. Be safe. Don't look up. Just run like hell till you reach the back gate."

I nodded. Mr. Adhikari had explained to me in detail the insides of the Taj - how to get from the back gate to the rooms where Apu could be, without hopefully getting noticed. If anyone stopped me, hoping it was not a terrorist, I had to pretend to be a guest searching desperately for my wife.

"If I don't-"

Gill Uncle stopped me. "You will." He gestured towards Taj. "Run. Apu's waiting."

"Thanks," I mouthed to him silently. Then another thanks to Mr. Adikari. I put my phone on silent. Then I crossed my heart and plunged.

Mumbai, Nov 27, 2008, 3:40 PM

It was a short long journey. From the gate near the pool to the basement, then into ankle deep water that had flooded the area. Then up the flooded fire-escape stairs against the rushing, noisy water. The stairs circled around a central column so that each floor was made up of four set of stairs. I climbed them slowly, alert for any interruption.

I had made it two floors up when suddenly there was a loud noise to my right. A split second later, before I could understand what happened, a gust of thick, dark smoke filled with debris particles hit me. My eyes burned. Blind, I coughed with my hand upon my mouth, trying to choke my own sound. The stairs were wet, and as I thrashed about trying to expel the poisonous smoke, I slipped and rolled down the stairs.

Curled at the bottom, when I tried to get up, I couldn't. There was an excruciating pain in my left side. Waves of tingling surged through my leg. What had happened? Did I break a bone or something during the fall?

I looked down. I saw a dark stain getting bigger on my left flank, the water flowing past getting suffused with red.

Guess I was… shot?xxx

Mumbai, Nov 27, 2008, 3:54 PM

Minutes later, I had managed to drag myself up to a sitting position against the wall. While I tried to keep myself focused and to figure out what to do, my phone vibrated. It was… APU!

I felt a chilling fear. Who was calling from her phone? Wasn't it…

I pressed the accept button and took the phone to my ear slowly.

It was Apu speaking! My heart jumped. I could hear her whispering my name. I couldn't believe it! She *was* alive!

"Apu!"

"Ani!"

"Apu!"

I tried getting up but I couldn't. "Apu!"

"Ani!" she said urgently this time. "Yes, I am alive. Now will you stop repeating my name and listen to me? I am not *out* yet. But I know where I am now."

"I am sorry." I guess I was crying her name from relief again and again.

"Are you listening Ani?"

I clenched my hands and tried to focus. Bloody pain. "Yes… sorry baby. Where *are* you?" I had a little difficulty breathing.

She didn't answer the question. "Ani, are you ok?"

"Yes, I am ok!" I blustered, as loudly as I could. "It's you who are not ok! Why you asking?"

"I thought I heard you gasp. You seemed in pain!"

"I… Will you stop wasting time Apu?" I replied harshly to deflect her attention from me. "We need to get to you. You said you know where you are. Where?"

"Sorry," she deflated. "Yes. I have run to a different room. Number's 229."

"But how did you– " Then I stopped myself. There was no time for stories. Could I get to her room? I was close to the first floor and her room couldn't be far away. I tried getting up again, but such a wave of pain shot through me that I fell back, barely stifling a cry of agony.

I looked down; I was still bleeding. Hopefully slowly. I had no choice but to call Rohan.

"Wait I'll put you on conference with Rohan," I told Apu. "He's in touch with the hotel helpline."

Fortunately, she didn't ask any questions. She just said: "Quick… please."

As soon as Rohan picked up the phone, and before he could say anything and give away where I was, I gritted my teeth and spoke. "Rohan… Apu's in room 229! She's also on the line. I have put you on conference call."

There was a moment's silence. Then Rohan yelled back. "Apu! You're alive!"

"Yes!" said my wife. "And in room 229."

"My God! Aaru… Apu Bhabhi's safe!" we heard Rohan yelling euphorically and running towards the room where I guess everyone else was. Seconds later, we heard him again. "Wait! I'll put you on speaker Apu. Apu… everyone's here," Rohan was saying in the speaker. "Jerry, Uncle, Auntie, Aaru… everyone. We are all waiting for you Apu. To come home Apu."

Apu said "hi", her voice full of happiness. She sounded as if she was not trapped in a terrorist filled hotel, but holidaying in Europe. "Waiting to come home too," she said.

How had this happened? How did she turn so positive? I wanted to cheer loudly for my girl if it were not for the intense pain in my stomach and the cold water flowing past me and through me and the horrible shivering and the desire to just curl up and go to sleep.

I couldn't cheer, but others were expressing their happiness in their own ways. I heard Aaru make a choking sound. Someone, maa I guess, sniffled. And then before anyone else could say anything, there was a bellow. It was Jerry. "APU! APU!" he yelled again and again, crying, relieved, ecstatic, like me, like all of us, that his daughter was alive.

And then, what I had wished for a long time, happened... Dad gently put his arm around Jerry's shoulder and I heard his deep voice, filled with emotion, heavy, say to my girl. "Yes, come home beti. We have been waiting to see you for so long. I am so sorry that-"

My heart swelled with joy. The coldness and the pain seemed to fly away.

"Thanks dad," I mouthed to the phone silently. Hoping he had felt my thanks even though I knew he hadn't heard it.

Then I turned my face upwards and thanked god too. Told him even if I didn't make it today, I had no complaints.

I wished I could make it. Though.

I looked down. The water flowing past me continued to color deeply.

Mumbai, Nov 27, 2008, 3:59 PM

"Rohan, can you put me off the speaker phone and go out of the room," Apu said suddenly, cutting everyone's expressions of relief and happiness midway. "I have to talk to you alone."

That was a strange request!

"But-"

"It's urgent!" Her voice was calm... deadly calm. Businesslike. And urgent - far more than the word itself. "I am sorry... papa, dad, maa... But I *have* to talk to Rohan. I will talk to you guys later."

Fear gripped my heart. What was it that she did not want them to know?

Her voice was undeniable. "Gimme a second," Rohan said.

"Ok."

"Apu, what-" I began.

But she cut me. "Rohan, are you out of the room now?"

"Yes."

"Ani, I am cutting you too baby," she told me. "Talk to you later. Rohan, I am calling you *now*. Wait for it."

"But-"

She had cut the phone.

Shit! I forgot all my pain. If I could only get up.

Five seconds later, my phone began to vibrate again. It was Rohan! I picked up and heard Apu in mid-sentence. "... tell anyone. Not Ani, not dad, no one. Don't want everyone worrying again. Just get me help. Promise?"

"Ok," Rohan said.

Apu had no idea Rohan had dialed me in the call. She thought she was talking to him alone. Attaboy, my best friend! I wanted to hug him.

"How soon can it come?" Apu asked.

"I will have the helpline send commandos immediately," Rohan told her.

"How soon?"

"I don't know for sure. Fifteen… twenty minutes."

"I hope I have that much time."

"What happened?"

"There is fire outside the door. It had gone down earlier, but now it's blazing again. No way I can get out. I have closed the door, but a bigger problem is the thick, dark smoke. It's coming through the top and sides."

As if on cue, Apu began coughing.

"Why didn't you say this before? Every minute was crucial!"

"I was trying to find the right time… everyone was so happy. I couldn't."

"Ok, no matter. I am calling the helpline," Rohan said. "You hold on. Ok."

"Ok."

"And Ani's on the call too. Sorry, I connected him without telling you. Talk to him. He *has* the right to be worried!" He paused and switched to me. "Ani, meanwhile if you can get to-"

I cut him. Apu shouldn't know where I was now. "I am on it dude. You just get the commandos!"

"What?" Apu asked.

Thankfully, without waiting to answer Apu's question, Rohan logged off the call.

"It's nothing babe," I fibbed to her. "We were just trying to locate where you were."

"I am in 229."

"Yeah… we know that now."

"Ani! I am sorry I didn't want to tell you about the fire and smoke!

Didn't want you to worry-"

"That's ok."

Right then, Apu began coughing. Badly, really badly.

"What happened?"

"The ...moke... t's thickenin...." She wouldn't stop coughing.

"Put something on the door! Bed sheet maybe?... Towel? Towel! Can you find one?"

"I already have...."

There was a pause. "Ani, I think will have to break the window."

"Smoke's that bad?"

"Yes. Am standing on the bed now. Difficult to breathe."

Shit! I *had* to reach my wife now. I *had* to get up.

I laid my forearm flat on the bottom stair. The other hand held the mobile above the cascading water. Biting my lip, I leaned on my forearm as I drew my right leg back.

"Ani?" Apu's voice floated from the phone.

I brought my right leg back, slowly, till almost halfway. I breathed.

"Ani?"

Hold on Apu. I am coming. Pressing down on the stair with all my might, I now drew the left leg back, ignoring the pain that felt as if someone was pushing a burning spear up through my body. I rose a few inches. Seemed I could do it. A few more and I will push forward and fall down on my knee. And then I could get up.

"*Ani*?"

I clenched my teeth and brought the phone closer. "Yes."

"What happened? Where did you go?" Apu wheezed. She was breathing bad - heavily, erratically. F**k!

A few more inches. Yes.

"I was-"

And then it happened. My heel slipped. I lost control and my left leg sped forward, making me fall down again on my bottom with a hellish stab of pain that almost drew a scream out of me. I gnashed the scream down, tasting blood.

"Ani?"

It was impossible to speak for a few seconds, as I tried to orient myself through the unbearable pain. I looked down. Seemed I was losing blood faster now.

Suddenly, there was a big explosion nearby.

"What's *going* on Ani?"

"Nothing," I managed to fib to Apu. "Grenade came out of one of the windows. Far away. Policeman trying to control crowd... and I was making him not arrest me."

"Are you safe?"

"Forget about ME!"

Two minutes had gone from the precious few we had. She was no more than thirty-forty meters away from me, and yet I was nowhere close to helping Apu. Why was fate being so cruel?

God! Please help!

"Apu. What is there in the room to break the window?"

"There's an armchair. But I can't lift it. It's too heavy!"

"Try."

There was silence for about half a minute, punctuated by a series of small explosions somewhere in the hotel.

"I did. Can lift it a bit, but I can't get up to the win... ndow."

"TRY AGAIN!"

"Can't Ani! I am sorry."

And then she began coughing once more. Seemed like she was choking.

"Apu?"

I heard the continuous sound of heavy coughing. I pictured her beside the chair, doubled up, cringing on the floor.

"Apu! Leave the chair! Get on the bed!"

… … … … … … …

"GET UP!" I screamed with all my might.

And then her voice came on the phone, breathing heavily. "Yes… up. Am up."

"Stay with me baby!"

"Yes… yes… I will. Thanks."

"What else is there?"

"What?"

"To break the window. What else is there?"

There was a moment's silence.

"I can see a big glass paperweight."

"Try it."

"It's too small… but I'll try."

There were many small thuds in quick succession.

"Ani, not… it's not working!" Her voice came on the phone again. She was breathing harder than an asthmatic patient. "The glass is thick. It's not even got marked."

"You have to keep *trying*!"

"It's not much use. Don't see even a scr… scratch."

"You can't stop-"

She cut me. "Ani… I love you."

"STOP SAYING THAT!" I bellowed.

"Ani… listen-"

One astonishing thing struck me. Even now, Apu's voice was calm. Urgent, but calm.

I felt furious. This couldn't happen. Why can't I get up? Why can't she break the window? How could she be so calm? Why can't someone do *something*?

"YOU CAN'T STOP!" I screamed between the hot tears burning my eyes. "WHAT ELSE IS THERE IN THE ROOM?"

… … … … … … … …

"APU! STAY WITH ME!"

"Ani… I love you."

"I AM NOT LETTING YOU GO. WHAT ELSE IS THERE? FIND OUT OR I AM COMING IN THERE. LET THEM KILL ME TOO!"

"NO!"

"Yes, I am coming in!"

"NO! STAY WHERE YOU ARE!"

"What *else* is there then? Tell me."

She was silent for about ten seconds. "Yes! There is a table…a glass-top table! I see it."

"Can you lift it?"

Silence again.

"Think I can… I can… It's heav… vy… but I can."

"GO FOR IT."

"Ok."

Soon, I heard a heavy thud. Then another. Another…

"This is not working either!"

"It will! Keep trying!"

"The glass seems as if it is bullet-proof!"

"Don't hit the glass then! Hit the frame, lock… something. YOU MUST!"

Thud. Thud.

Silence.

"APU!"

… … … … … … … …

"WHERE ARE YOU?"

… … … … … … … …

I could almost see her bent over the table, dead tired, smoke clogged, choking, about to lose consciousness.

"NO! GET UP!"

If there is god, then…

"APU!"

I was screaming more at *him*.

… … … … … … … …

"APU!"

Then it started again.

Thud. Thud.

Yes!

Thud. Thud. Thud. Thud.

THUD.

And then there was a yell. A yell of joy!

The handle lock had broken.

Mumbai, Nov 27, 2008, 4:17 PM

Apu was in a sparkling mood. She said she was hanging out of her window, breathing the fresh air. Almost laughing, almost herself. It felt as if I was talking to a girl altogether different from the one I had talked to in the morning.

"The baby kicked me." Her voice was jubilant, explaining how she managed call me even after her phone went dead. "There was lots of smoke and it was overwhelming me, and I had given up when it kicked me hard, really hard. It kicked me, again and again, and wouldn't stop. As if keeping me conscious, as if telling me to get up. And then I thought maybe it was actually god who was telling me I couldn't give up. You know… telling it through our baby. To get up. So I got up and went out and then suddenly, I saw the mobile lying on the table. It was gleaming through the smoke. I knew it was god's sign again, knew for certain why it was there. I took out its battery and put it in my phone and it started working. All fear was gone in that moment. I knew I would live because god was with me. He was just telling me to get my ass of the floor and help myself. That our baby and I were supposed to survive even if Dibbs hadn't. That I couldn't give up."

Apu asked me wasn't that amazing. It wasn't actually. Somewhere deep down I had always believed my girl, who had once decided to ride my Triumph to get me a doctor, would pull herself out of her despair and find a way to get out. But it wasn't the time to contradict her.

"Yes," I replied, my heart so full it was hard to speak. "So I guess I have one more person to thank now."

"Thank?"

"Our baby," I whispered.

Apu laughed loudly. “Oh yes! My baby, my savior. And *you*.”

I was about to scold her for being recklessly loud when I got a message from Rohan. “Get off phne dude! Helpline tryng to rech Apu. To send comandos. Now!”

I told Apu I had to go.

“Why?”

“The helpline has to get to you stupid! To send commandos. Don’t take anymore calls unless it is the helpline.”

“Okie. Will do that,” she whispered. ”Love you. And see you soon.”

“Love you too.”

“You will meet me right outside the hotel… right?”

“Yes,” I lied. “Near the Gateway. I will meet you there.” Then I cut the call.

A minute later, Rohan called me. I cut his call, not wanting anyone to find out about the situation I was in yet; I didn’t want their attention getting away from Apu. He called me again. I cut it again. Then I got a message from him telling me that if I was inside the hotel, I should get the hell out right now since help was going to reach Apu immediately.

I didn’t reply.

Mumbai, Nov 27, 2008, 4:32 PM

Apu to me: “Cmmandoes in my room. Me rescued. Yeah!!”

Yeah!

Me to Apu: “Gr8! Msg me as soon as u r out and safe.”

Apu to me: “I am already safe! But… okie. Will do ☺

I was happy, so happy. And extremely cold.

Mumbai, Nov 27, 2008, 4:46 PM

It was funny in a twisted way. I had come to rescue Apu and I was the one that needed a rescue (bigger) now. I was still losing blood. So I lay quietly on the stairs, my teeth chattering heavily, trying to keep myself conscious as I waited for Apu's message that she was out and safe. I had decided I would call up Gill Uncle after that.

Sometime later, as I was fighting off the blackness swallowing me, I heard footsteps and hushed voices. Seemed someone was coming down the stairs. Rather more than one person.

I stared upwards trying to figure out who they were. Slowly a masked face and a muzzle of a gun pointed straight at me came into view. The man yelled at me, but I couldn't understand him above the loud rush of water. I didn't have the strength to yell back, so I just pointed at my stomach hoping he would understand the gesture.

The man shouted something again. Bloody! Why couldn't I hear him? I gestured back once more, then stopped from exhaustion. I laid my head against the wall and closed my eyes. To hell with him.

Apu was safe. I didn't care anymore.

Then I heard him coming down. When it sounded as if he was almost next to me, I half-opened my eyes. I saw the gun was pointed at me still, its muzzle hovering a feet above. The man shouted again. This time I understood what he said.

But before I could answer him, I heard a terrifying scream.

Mumbai, Nov 27, 2008, 4:54 PM

"No!"

It was a woman's cry. The woman screamed again, and then I heard someone scrambling down the stairs as other manly voices yelled something in unison. A second later the guy standing above me yelled too. "Ma'am! Stay back!" he said.

"No! Let me go!" the woman cried. "Don't shoot him! That's my husband!"

I recognized the voice and jerked my eyes open. Slowly I turned my face towards the top of the stairs, and found myself looking once more at the toes of a pair of pretty feet clad in Kolhapuri chappals. It was impossible not to minutely notice the beige nail polish and the yellow toe-ring with silver beads on the third toe. Further inspection was interrupted by the owner who bent down and yelled at me: "What are *you* doing here?"

It was a charming voice as always. As my eyes moved up her body, I noticed other attributes in this order: soiled white salwar, really soiled white kameez streaked with blackish soot, blackish hands with green bangles and though I couldn't discern, I was sure they had the same beige nail polish I had noticed on the toes, long disheveled hair, svelte figure with a significant bulge in the stomach, green dupatta, nice... Politely, I removed my eyes from the round, tantalizing pair upwards... silvery necklace, full lips, nose a little flared and dirty, brown eyes with large lashes, and eyebrows like mine – slightly curving out, then smoothing down. My assister, as always, was pretty and was wearing super large ear rings.

I was surprised! She was coming out the same way I had planned to get to her!

I tried smiling at her.

Guess it didn't work. "What are you doing *here*?" she yelled again.

I wanted to tell her that I knew it did look *quite* far from that, but

I had actually come to *save* her.

But nothing would come out. Then Apu and the masked man began to disappear in whiteness. I closed my eyes and leaned back against the wall. It was so cold and my whole body seemed to have frozen. I could hear only faint, indistinct voices.

"... think he's hurt ma'am."

"What! Please help him!"

Take her with you. ...will come back... won't go... ma'am you must... please... help... will be here... Ani.

Then I heard one sentence clearly, whispered into my ear by a terrified Apu. "Stay with me Ani. *Stay*!"

I tried to open my eyes a little. I wanted to assure her that I would be ok now that she was here with me. And though I couldn't see anything, I smelled Apu, her familiar, comforting smell, speaking to me of a world that was warm, cozy, safe. Full of love and laughter. I felt her soft caress on my cheek. Then a fleeting touch of her lips on mine.

Her words. *Ani... you must... our baby...*

I gathered all my energy and stretched my eyes wider. Apu was blurred. But she was there. "Kiss me."

"Sshhh..."

"*Kiss me.*"

"Baby-"

"Supposed to... die kissing?" I tried to smile. "Didn't... you... tell me?"

"No! Shut up! Don't say such things!"

"Kiss me. I will."

I felt a large drop of warm tear fall on my eye. Then many more tears. "Why you had to play the hero? You knew it was dangerous!"

I sighed. "No... point in... living... you couldn't get out."

"No!" she cried pressing her hand on my lips. "Don't say that! You'll be ok by tomorrow I know."

I tried to lift my right hand. "C... come here."

"No! You're hurt!"

I ignored her. "Want... lean... on... you. Love... you."

That did the trick. Apu smiled through the tears. She shuffled forward and leaned towards me. "Love you too."

Gingerly, she put her arms around me. And we kissed.

Forever this way.

Somebody spoke. I heard him faintly. "Ma'am... take hospital..."

Her lips left me. She was withdrawing. No. I tried to clutch at her. Lips... chin... a finger...

Apu.

Then there was darkness.

Delhi, Nov 27, 2009

Our entire family got together and sat down with Apu to eat Peking Duck, finishing the meal she had started a year earlier with Dibbs. Rohan and Gill Uncle swayed everyone to come – it would be a tribute to the dead they said. Even the vegetarians (meaning maa and Dad) took some gravy.

Midway through the dinner, Apu told everyone that I was also there - sitting next to Dibbs. And then she began to cry.

Maa rushed to comfort her, crying herself. Of course no one believed

Apu, thinking she was hallucinating - talking of seeing ghosts. The pain of a bereaved wife.

But it's true. It was the best meal we ever had – me and Dibbs. Smiling, happy, hogging the Pecking Duck more than anyone else, we sat there flashing Apu a victory sign now and then.

Also in Apu's lap was our eight month old son. Named Aniruddh after his dad, he slept quietly in his mother's arms.

We had won.